THE MI**S**ING
IN**DIA**
MURDERS

Gauri Sinh is the former Editor of *Bombay Times*, the lifestyle and entertainment supplement of *The Times of India,* and *After Hrs*, the lifestyle and entertainment supplement of DNA. She has written numerous popular columns on lifestyle and entertainment for both broadsheets, as well as on social issues and parenting for DNA. In the past, she also edited youth magazines *Femina Girl* and JLT. Her two previous books are *Dogsend, the story of Simba* (2010) and *The Garud Prophecies, Sitara's story* (2015). Gauri lives and works in Mumbai. Her website is www.gaurisinh.com.

THE MISS INDIA MURDERS

GAURI SINH

HARPER
BLACK

First published in India in 2018 by HarperBlack
An imprint of HarperCollins *Publishers*
A-75, Sector 57, Noida, Uttar Pradesh 201301, India
www.harpercollins.co.in

2 4 6 8 10 9 7 5 3 1

P-ISBN: 978-93-5277-587-3
E-ISBN: 978-93-5277-588-0

Typeset in 11/13.6 Minion Pro at
Manipal Digital Systems, Manipal

Printed and bound at
Thomson Press (India) Ltd

A murder mystery full of girls, gloss, gore and ghouls (!)
for the most important men in my life, all of whom love a
tale with a twist!

Papa
*A whodunnit saga from daddy's not-so-little girl for her papa,
because he's bestest. And because I have an answer now for the
continuing 'phir kya hua' family legend!*

Chaitanya
*Wrote a story about glamourettas, but eternally thrilled to be
Cheerleader Number One of your ever-increasing fan club, you
lead by example so.*

and

Gautam
*Front page pieces in a national paper that was pink, (how
did I do it, the 'showpiece of the family'?) and now a story
featuring several such showpieces—dedicated to you! How
the unmighty have risen from lovin' candyfloss pink! Or then,
because the love of a brother, teasing or protective, is most
important in the grand scheme of things*

Prologue
Akruti

'FAB-ULOUS! To die for!' Sharmila Kapadia, choreographer for this year's pageant, bellows into the mic, sounding highly appreciative as Niamat executes a perfect turn on the ramp. Niamat's face flushes with pleasure—I can see it even at this distance.

I am so fond of Niamat. She is after all, my niece, the reason I am here in the family enclosure, watching this rehearsal-in-progress for the Miss India pageant 2018. Niamat is delighted to have me here watching. Her favourite auntie Aku, the most glamorous one in the family, she says.

I watch her closely, my sharp pride quite evident. Niamat wants this crown bad, it is obvious. I am thrilled at this open flaunting of her determination to best all, ambition is always healthy.

But, 'to die for'? Can beauty really be that? And I am reminded of another time, another contest. I was barely twenty then, younger than Niamat is now. But it was where it all began, my current career.

I wasn't *the* Akruti Rai then, not the way I am now. Though I thought I was, then, you see. Because I was already the country's number one model, enjoying all the trappings that come with that kind of success.

In fact, I had known fame very young, very fast; even before the Miss India pageant began. The Miss India title was to be the crowning glory of my achievements; a stepping stone, not just to bigger recognition on world stage, but also, to filmdom.

I was in such a hurry to have it all, spoiled by what came early and without fuss. I had it planned. We tend so, towards a sense of entitlement when we taste unadulterated success. Instant celebrity without necessary toil allows us to believe ourselves invincible. And then, when it starts to go horribly wrong, we feel cheated, deprived, as if life itself has dealt us a cruel blow without warning.

Though really, there was an awful lot that went wrong, and gruesomely so, in that particular Miss India pageant. I wonder if it was sheer bumbling luck that things turned out as they did in the end. It is quite a story. Let me tell it, so you can decide for yourself.

Four days to the finale …

1

Akruti

'BEGIN,' Avi called out, imperious, and the music streamed through. It reverberated across the stage, thunderous in the open-air auditorium. Lajjo, uncharacteristically, had already begun walking towards me from her position at base ramp. She was almost at midpoint, though her walk and the music should have commenced simultaneously. It was unlike her to be so eager, to defy Avi's meticulous cueing and choreography.

She swayed to the sonorous march, jerked once. A trifle ungraceful, that movement, but her catwalk was still sensuous. She sashayed up the ramp to join me at the very top. As she passed the ramp's midway point, I turned, backing her advance, facing the audience seats now.

The nineteen other contestants held positions as she passed each, edging both sides of the long ramp in formation. I was alone right at the top, 'head ramp' in fashion parlance, waiting with the rest. Lajjo deliberately stretched time, using it to call attention to herself. Slow, languorous, her advance. Both she and I knew how precious time on centre stage could be. The lights had faded on cue to be replaced by a lone singular spotlight on her as she walked.

Finally I heard her step behind me. It was precisely timed, though my back was to her and I faced the audience—I

5

needed to sense her arrival, turn automatically to join her. Do this without missing a beat, as if I had eyes at the back of my head. A complicated ramp move, only very experienced models got it correct. Avi, master choreographer, had immense confidence I would not fail him in this, and so far, at every rehearsal, I had proved him right.

Now too, I heard her arrival, over the beating drums of the musical march, though today it seemed a bit misplaced, her timing. I turned to face her. We were to match steps. But instead of turning with me, to peel away from centre as we had been taught, she stopped abruptly. We stood facing each other for a split second, centre stage. Bathed in the spotlight, my heartbeat echoed the drum roll of the music in that moment, every sense on high alert. What was Lajjo upto?

I can see her now, as she looked at that moment—face a mask, eyebrows arched, as if startled. I was taking it all in as if suspended in time. A moment of acute, febrile intensity because she was behaving so oddly: her surprised face, the sweat-patch dark and sticky on the front of her red velvet gown. 'What she's wearing is much too tight, perspiration shouldn't be showing so severely on it,' I had thought, slightly repulsed at the sight.

Then, as if in slow motion, her body toppled forward, collapsing onto mine, heavy in fall despite her slight form. I held her as she fell, my reaction automatic, noting in deep shock my hands reddening where they touched her bodice as they extended to catch her. That's when it hit me violently, the stark horror of it—that wasn't sweat on the front of her dress. It was blood, masked by the deep red velvet colour of the gown.

'CUT the music, spot. FULL LIGHTS!' blared Avi from the sound console a distance away, clearly in a rage because his stars hadn't come through, obviously unaware of what had just occurred in the very midst of his precious sequence.

That was when I saw the blade. We all did, flashing silver in the harsh glare of the just-turned on stage lights. So thin it looked like a paper cutter, the light glinting off its metallic grip-edge. Only the handle showed, intricately carved, quite breath-taking as weapons go, I thought later. I couldn't help thinking I'd seen that handle somewhere, but at that moment, it escaped me. The rest of the blade was in Lajjo's back, driven clean through her with great force, so it had nearly come out the other side, causing the blood to flow with such abandon that I had thought it sweat.

Lajjo, beautiful sensual Lajjo, the contestant labelled 'Hot Chocolate' for her lovely colour. The contestant I once thought most likely to win the crown if I didn't, had now toppled over, lifeless on head ramp ... Just moments back, Avi, in great admiration, had declared how her grace 'killed' him.

And here she was now, in grievous juxtaposition to his words, actually *killed*. Slain in a horrific, gory way, as in a bad horror movie. Audaciously, theatrically killed, with a carved silver blade in her back and blood all over the place. 'Murder? At the Miss India pageant?' I remember thinking, incredulous, as I held on to her, even in deep shock. Then pandemonium broke loose.

But let me go back a bit. It had started out as an ordinary day. Well, not that ordinary, considering that it was the Miss India 1995 pageant, a national contest. We were all finalists, vying for the crown and the attention and the considerable prize money that followed.

But ordinary as far as the contest was concerned—just another day of rehearsals. There were more nerves amongst us today, though. We were, after all, only four days away from the big day. Today we were rehearsing the sequence in gowns.

'You kill me, really, you do!' Avi's voice had shrilled over the microphone, the pleasure in his cackle evident, even over the soaring crescendo of the penultimate strains of 'Sabse khubsurat tum hi', the chosen soundtrack for the finale sequence at the rehearsal. I recognized this particular timbre in Avi's voice. I had heard it countless times, over so many years, in all our earlier ramp shows together. The strain of all-out effort giving in to deep pride as vision married the moment. And he foresaw in the now, a glimpse of the greatness of what might occur, if this very scenario recreated itself on D-Day.

Avi was all about the moment—getting it perfect, and getting all the credit for it later. As India's top choreographer and event manager, he worked hard and seldom praised any model or star, save his pets, and everyone in the industry knew who they were. To all the rest (make that the rest of India), which included anyone who knew the beauty industry— they were the best in the business. Avi only ever concerned himself with the best. Like him, his pets too were mostly about getting everything right the first time; as if they could control the outcome. Mistakes were costly, and inconvenient to everybody—on ramp, in life. Better avoided if they could be, was his motto. And his charmed coterie swore by it.

'Just, like that, hold for applause. RELEASE!' Avi continued, concentration intense, senses honed, as if in preparation for the praise that was inevitable, given such fluid posture.

He was addressing Lajwanti Khan of course, lissom and languid on head ramp, like a graceful cat. Front and centre, posing as if she owned it, simpering at his words, as if she knew they were aimed particularly at her. She wasn't alone; the other contestants, nineteen of them in fact, swamped her slender figure on both sides, edging the ramp in two lines behind her, all the way to stage. But it was justified, her arrogance. They knew it as well as she did. Even in the mammoth open air amphitheatre full of people connected to the contest, with the microphone echoing his every word to any who chose to listen—Avi had been talking only to her.

Her pose at the head of ramp eclipsed all those behind her. A feast for the eyes and senses, calling to mind a regal goddess living the moment granted her to the hilt. If she managed as seamless an execution at the finale itself … but I didn't want to think so far ahead yet.

'Avi, how is this?' she asked, miming her sentence as she changed stance, exaggerating each word through expression, because Avi, at the sound console so far away, couldn't hear her voice above the music. Obviously one didn't need to look at Avi's emphatic thumbs-up to know it was perfect, her form.

Lajwanti, or 'Lajjo', as we'd come to address her this past fortnight of training for the crown, was a diva. Make that Diva, with a capital D. She had done a few shows in her hometown of Hyderabad, but not enough to bring national recall to her name. Still, though she hadn't reached the top quite yet, her confidence now made her seem as if she would soon.

In this pageant, she seemed incandescent, her sureness and poise and undoubtedly Avi's whimsical favour winning her many votes in the smaller pre-contests leading up to the crown. She had grace and presence, along with the self-assurance that marks out a winner. She dearly wanted the crown, just as I did.

Let me add a bit of milieu to this aspiration we shared. Print ads circa 1995, the year we were in, more often than not featured those with milky white complexions. Also, if you had light eyes, it rather helped. Our world was one of illusion. Catering to market forces as it did, its reality was practical, if heart breaking in its irony. And whilst the hypocrisy (we are after all, a nation of more dark skin and eyes, than light) was awful, I was nothing if not a survivor. The rules were partial to my looks at the time, I milked the situation. And my rise as a glamour model was instant and legendary, first in print glossies, and television advertising, then, as I was noticed nationally, in ramp shows.

I wasn't tall, not Amazonian like that girl Parvati Samant in this pageant, certainly not as tall as Lajjo herself. But I made the cut at 5' 7". Sure, I had presence, and choreographers liked my sass. They also liked my instant recognizability, and thus marketability. So, I was 'discovered' as a ramp talent too, by Avi—Avinash Mahadeo—choreographer extraordinaire, as I knew him then, and together, we quickly became a startling success. No show was complete without us.

Most would call my rise to fame unbelievably quick—I had never really known much struggle. Nor the dark underbelly (falling prey to charlatans, or the casting couch) that could, and often did, cripple many ambitions of fledglings in the glamour business. The press, in fact, happily cemented my soaring career status with the title 'nation's sweetheart' when they wrote of me. This transition—from newbie to super success, and the resulting press moniker— occurred so smoothly I assumed it a given with every new assignment.

There is a certain innocence that reveals itself, that cocoons a person when a rise is devoid of bitter struggle, devoid of the disillusion of compromise. So it was with me. I was young, successful, untarnished by any major hardship.

You might wonder at this point in my narrative, given all I had achieved, and so very early, why I would be interested in a beauty pageant title at all.

I have a one word answer for that question: films. I had conquered all three mediums—print, TV, ramp as a model fairly painlessly, and very young. To my mind, then, my next natural step was films.

But being an established name in the modelling business at the time was often not enough to have Bollywood's dream merchants sit up and take note of you. Unlike today, the two industries operated quite independent of each other. Yet if you managed to transcend the catwalk, somehow got yourself into instant recall mode with most of India—why then, the movie business was happy to align itself with you. National visibility meant instant recall.

Thus in the 1990s, if you didn't come from a B-Town family, or have an established Godfather therein, the easiest way to enter the movies was via a national beauty pageant.

Hence my presence here, at this Miss India 1995 pageant, despite having tasted intense, absolute success in the glamour stakes already. Did I ever consider the possibility of losing the Miss India title to another— worse—a novice? Did it cross my mind even once, the hit my supernova career would take, were I somehow to fail in this venture? I would be lying if I said no.

But here's the thing—the benefit of competing still outweighed the risk of losing. There was no easier way to propel my career forward to tinsel town. Given that I had already bested all that modelling had to offer, I would stagnate without the momentum this contest promised. I figured I was prepared for the challenge, as equipped as I'd ever be. I hadn't failed so far, why hesitate now? My confidence only underlined my untainted upward trajectory—I was never more ready for greener pastures than at this time.

And my ambition wasn't subtle by any standards. The morning papers were proof enough of that—the lifestyle glossies loved that I had entered the contest this year, and splashed story upon story almost daily, all featuring me. The mega media conglomerate, *Eye India,* which owned the contest, loved the publicity my visibility built up. It was win-win for everybody. All I needed was the crown.

Lajjo, meanwhile, hadn't had as meteoric a rise as I, even though she had been a model as well, before entering the pageant. Her dusky complexion might have had to do with the sparse success in print and on TV, though secretly, I envied her unblemished chocolate smooth skin, so different from mine. Now I watched Lajjo's play for Avi's attention.

Lajjo might have remained an underground sensation, a wonder only in her hometown, had it not been for the ramp world. Unlike print and television, the catwalk in India followed its own rules. And height and gait had paramount importance, held more sway certainly, than skin colour— which to me seemed more egalitarian.

You cannot change what you are born with, but you can stand up straighter, give the impression of being tall. And you can work on your walk, so as to appear elegant. Needless to say, a majority of the reigning catwalk stars were therefore, and blessedly so, dark-skinned.

Noyna, Svetna, Shital, Carolle, Netra … they didn't need their last names to be recognized, they were known by just their first. All firmly established and sought-after on ramp, their skin a burnished brown. Whether this was thumbing their noses to the suits who dictated ads on TV and print, or whether it was just a sign of those times, a massive consensual effort by designers, choreographers and the ramp industry at large—it was gratifying to see. Because honestly, it can get monotonous if everyone I walk with on stage looks exactly like me.

So here we were, Lajjo and I, both products of our ambition and our age. And then, it was the best of times for the contest itself. 1994 had seen two Miss India winners win international titles. Their victory thrust both the national pageant and the media conglomerate into the world's gaze.

On national stage, recent liberalization meant international brands, and with them endorsements and ad campaigns, would be winging their way into the county soon enough. The world's eyes were on us. It was the heyday for glamour pageants and the fashion and beauty industry in India. And we couldn't be happier, because it meant a wider professional reach, were we to win yet again on the international stage.

Keeping this in mind, this year, the year immediately succeeding the big wins abroad, *Eye India* had spared no expense to razzle-dazzle and upscale the proceedings. It would be a contest like no other, we had been assured of it by our minders, all representatives of the company. A made-for-television spectacle as well, thrillingly extravagant and broadcast live all over the country.

The girls twitched impatiently on stage. Everyone looked a bit put out by Avi's clear singling out of Lajjo. Rehearsals for any show were always long and intense, but this time there was a crown at stake. And today, after a gruelling two-and-a-half-weeks of training, there were only four days left and paranoia had replaced pragmatism amongst us all, Avi included. Nerves were very much on display, it was after all a huge production, to be telecast live as well. We couldn't afford glitches.

For those of us already deeply established in the fashion world, our reputations rode on the outcome of this pageant. Lajjo and I were the only professional models contesting. But there was also Avi, and the sound and technical team, the backstage team, photographers, the makeup and hair personnel. There were other assorted professionals who put it all together and mentored the contestants. And then of course, there was the megalith media conglomerate, *Eye India* itself, and its television partners (the World Wide Web was still in the not-so-distant future, and live streaming hadn't yet become reality)—old hands, all, with careers and soaring status' to protect.

Avi's clear favour of Lajjo was annoying me as well. I was intensely aware that though Lajjo hadn't reached quite as far as me professionally in the glamour business, tomorrow is another day. You are only as good as your last gig.

I was acutely conscious of this, especially as the finale drew nearer. As I was sure Avi was, else he wouldn't have been so effusive in his praise, knowing that I was watching everything, and that I was up next. I knew in the glamour stakes, appearance is all. And so, my move to counter her, immediate and decisive, loud enough over the music so everyone heard.

'Aviiinash,' I trilled, elongating the I in the name, a measured effort to show both ownership and a deliberate if affectionate pique at his favour diverted so, to any other than I. 'When is my cue to walk?'

Avi turned from the sound console, clearly distracted by the subtle warning of temper in my tone. Avi was all about nuance, which is part of what made him such a gifted choreographer. I had always been his star model, we had created a certain magic together. There was history between us enough times for the industry to brand me his protégé on ramp. But I knew, as Avi did, that in modelling, as in business, there are no permanent friendships and no permanent enmity. In a world driven so by illusions— creating them, sustaining them, selling them—it is always and utterly—about just that moment. Clearly this moment wasn't mine and I was having none of it. As always, Avi rushed to placate. Till the crown was decided, I was still Queen Bee, notwithstanding upstarts.

'Akrrruti, Darrrrling,' he purred, rolling the Rs in conciliation. 'Could there be a finale without your entry? Come, love, get on the stage …'

It wasn't as if we weren't aware of our finale positions or cues or even entry points. But today, four days to D-Day, Avi had decided to experiment with music. This morning, all of a sudden, he had decided to use 'Sabse' instead of our regular track for this sequence. As our stage entry cues were always set to music, his unexpected change had thrown us all a bit off our game. Hence my query, firm and loud enough for Avi to hear, even over the music's megawatt boom.

I rose from my seat in the audience chairs, empty at present, where I had been sitting all this while, reading my cue sheet. The Miss India ramp walk wasn't all that different from the fashion shows I had done so far and I, being established already, was sometimes given a bit of leeway. Today, for instance, I had been allowed to sit up-front during rehearsals rather than wait in the wings backstage for my turn. In any case, I wasn't ever about subtlety.

'Watch this, Avi,' I simpered over the thudding soundtrack.

Then I walked up the six stairs in front leading straight to ramp from the audience seating, rather than entering from the stage area as I had normally done, as we had been practising all this while. Today my ego was taking liberties. I knew Avi wouldn't dare intervene, because like countless times in past shows together, he understood my current mood, my need to upstage all others present. Avi got nuances right every single time, he could read his star performers' minds like a book. Besides, he knew when I was like this, I would always be courting drama. For the stage, for live ramp shows—well, there's nothing quite like drama, even in an improvised avatar.

I was deliberately sashaying, giving the movement my A-game, though really it wasn't required right now. But I needed Lajjo to understand who was in the lead here. Upon reaching ramp, I turned to face her, letting my eyes, their colour so much lighter, *colder* in the halo of the spotlight, give her the full score of hauteur. 'I need some space,' I mouthed.

Lajjo's nostrils flared when I addressed her, incandescent skin even more aglow in the spotlight. We faced each other, opposite ends of the same ambition, light and dark, her Amazonian figure in six-inch heels dwarfing mine, though I too was in vertiginous, nose-bleed pumps, having shown my ramp prowess climbing those stairs effortlessly in these self-same shoes two seconds ago.

My unscripted, fifteen-second climb hadn't gone unnoticed by anyone who understood fashion. It is always harder than it looks, to negotiate stairs in high heels, especially whilst wearing tight gowns that barely allow for any leg movement. All those in the glamour world understand this well, all novices, even more so.

Trainers, choreographers and the like devoted intense sessions over several days getting contestants to look blithe and unconcerned all the while maintaining audience eye contact, ever smiling, as they negotiated each rung in dangerously high spikes. Fancy acrylic stages or stairwells, though they presented better for big performances, were often more difficult to manoeuvre, slipping on such surfaces was a constant and ready fear. One foot wrong and it was over for a shot at the crown. Worse, injuries could be nasty via stairwell tumbles.

Consequently, my little sashay up those stairs had managed to evoke both admiration and attention all around. It was clear I had the moment's psychological advantage, despite Lajjo's towering over me. And I had the stage, as Avi screeched over the mic, instantly attentive, demanding perfection. 'Lajwanti, please return to the formation once you've pirouetted, as in your cue sheet. Akruti, take centre stage—head ramp, please. You end the sequence, as always.'

Lajjo's eyes shot daggers as she acquiesced to Avi, though her face in sharp contrast, stayed serene, a beatific cinnamon Madonna, ever-professional. I refrained from gloating at this obscure victory. It was after all so petty, even if necessary in this game of thrones. My face matched hers in serenity as I glided into the spot she vacated on head ramp, front and centre, letting the light catch my profile—as if born to be here.

She would soon be joining me again for the final bow, doubling back as I finished my turn, followed by the rest, so audiences would see two lines peeling off, bang-smack centre, separating onto either side of ramp at head ramp. But for now the moment was mine. It was show time.

'Sabse's soaring climax filtered over the sound system, fitting end to a sequence that might ultimately play decider as to who went home with the crown. I got to end it—it was my face the judges would see last, thus recall first whilst tallying points, even though this sequence would not be included in the judging round. My professional success and Avi's support had got me this far. The rest was up to me.

'Spot cut … music lowered, and FADE!' Avi bellowed over the microphone, as we held the formation. Instant blackout descended. For thirty seconds, in pitch dark we had to hold our poses, incase the live TV cameras were still rolling, as they would be on the finale day. Then, as the lights and sound came on, Lajjo would join me on head ramp from her lone position at base stage, the first mover in a chain, so we could file out in decorum, still in formation.

Upon reaching the edge of stage, blackout once more, then run, still in these absurd heels without bumping into each other or tripping over garments to change for the announcement of the winners proceeding to the next round.

Today there was a lone camera mimicking the one we'd have at the finale, its red light blinking in the darkness from beyond head ramp as it captured us. We weren't to move backstage after the second blackout either. We would be waiting for Avi's instructions.

'LIGHTS!' Avi barked into the mic, and obligingly the stage was aglow again. We turned to each other, still in formation, two lines edging ramp, two stars at opposite ends—me at head ramp, Lajjo at the base of stage, waiting to join me.

'BEGIN!' shouted Avi, but Lajjo had already pre-empted the music and Avi's instructions, excruciating when I recall it now, her slow sashay towards me. And this was when it all started to go horribly wrong.

2
Akruti
‿

'Blood, blood, blood!' Myra, the contestant standing closest to us, began babbling hysterically as Lajjo toppled. Chaos followed. Three of the girls fainted, two began screaming wildly, gasping loudly for air between shrieks. The rest began exclaiming, some weeping in great heaving sobs, as the shock hit.

As I remember, I was still holding my arch-rival's inert body with the blade driven deep, its handle sticking out from her back when someone stepped up. Someone much taller than me, someone with clear brown eyes and a steady gaze, someone who had seemed intensely level-headed to me during training these past few weeks, that quality a necessary Godsend now.

'Let me help you,' the statuesque Parvati Samant said, easing Lajjo's passive form out of my hands, her calm words balm to my overwrought mind. 'Clear the area, please,' she added, this time to the rest of the contestants, her sudden, easy authority a revelation to me—I'd thought her something of a passive type all this while.

From the little I knew of Parvati over these two-and-a-half weeks of training, I understood her to be someone not given to moments of high drama. In fact, she had seemed understated in all she did, I had noted that, and even considered it a drawback at the time. In a contest such as this, one needed to let it all hang out, put everything on display, in wide angle 70 mm colour, I felt.

But in life, at some point, there comes a time when you are grateful, truly grateful to have someone low-key and level-headed by your side. This was undoubtedly one such moment, and I couldn't have been more grateful to have her there—an oasis of calm amidst the screeching, screaming banshees around. 'Thank God for the discreet, sensible ones,' I said to myself.

Parvati straightened from Lajjo's inactive figure, steady gaze locked into mine, mouthing what I already knew, 'She's gone.'

I nodded sombrely. There wasn't much to say at that point, the wailing around us was deafening in itself. Together we placed Lajjo on the floor of the ramp, face downwards so as not to drive the blade in further. The whole situation seemed surreal. Any moment now, I expected Lajjo to sit up and laugh, bizarrely denying she was dead, saying it was a joke of course. I was in shock I knew, with this fantasy—but I refused to crumple like the others. I was made of sterner stuff. Besides, Parvati seemed composed and I wouldn't let myself lose control if she was showing such fortitude.

'Move, girls,' I echoed her, suddenly spurred to action. I needed to *do* something, to not give myself time to *think*. 'Let's get off the ramp,' I said, then to the nearest minder, 'Someone please call the closest hospital. We'll need a doctor.'

Where was Avi in all this? The fashion industry to me, always operated best when under pressure. Many of its brightest lights—designers, choreographers, co-ordinators— furiously translated bursts of nebulous creativity into finite saleability or high art at a stressful pace. But such intense effort often took a toll. So many were high strung and nervy, comfortable only around what they knew and understood. Unsure in unfamiliar situations, many could and did unravel at the first sign of outside pressure. Not Avi though—he actually became the opposite at this time. It was now, in this unprecedented, unscripted and terrifically tragic moment, that Avi, master of rehearsed perfection, came completely into his own.

When the lights were switched on, he had gotten a glimpse of Lajjo, the knife in her back, the blood, her expression. My stricken face as I held her had told him what the white noise of contestants wailing and screeching a split second later, could not. Even as he pushed the sound console mic away, even without a doctor present to confirm the same, I could tell he knew Lajjo was gone.

Knowing Avi as well as I did, I realized that his hyper-sharp instinct was already at work. It was telling him, I was certain, that this was both a sordid and serious state of affairs. He hadn't bothered with sheparding the contestants, he knew their minders would step in. He wisely asked his aide to make an immediate call first to a hospital, then to the CEO of *Eye India*. I understood Avi's reasoning perfectly. Had he called the CEO himself, he would have had to give a long drawn out and detailed explanation, waste precious seconds.

Then, over and above the fashion world's ready superficiality, over and above consequences of not reporting in to the moolah-controlling bosses first, and in a sincere effort to do right by a girl he had believed a winner—he called the Mumbai police.

To me, the promptness of Avi's action was a fine show of real character—when I look back upon how quickly he reacted, and with such utter conviction, I really am proud to be called his protégé. Time is always of essence in righting wrongs effectively, and as one who understood the difference a second could make to any entry, on stage or off, it seemed to me that Avi had pulled off something miraculous. In an event as mammoth, as micro-managed as this one, he had, just by the one call, introduced an outside element to the proceedings. An unknown variable in a production tightly controlled, unforgivingly in-group, the group being a media behemoth, already all about image control from the word 'go'.

With his timely move, there was no scope for discussion, no cover up or the like entertained—might well have been attempts, had the *Eye India* bosses got involved first. After all, so much was riding on this event, publicity, revenue, reputations, the pageant was a national treasure at the very least.

'Minders. Step in, please. Take the girls off-stage,' Avi announced once over the mic, brusque, then stepped down, off the console to disappear at the far end. No doubt he would be alerting the hotel at the venue, the personnel on the premises to draw a veil over this incident where other guests were concerned, at once. It was now a matter for the authorities.

Because the police were called immediately, there was a better chance at unravelling the mystery behind Lajjo's gruesome end—the scene of crime was still fresh, untampered with, as was whatever went, by way of evidence. I didn't know this so well then, not at all, infact. But I'm narrating now with hindsight 20/20, adding these little extras, so it makes sense for you.

Without company safeguards or protocol in place, with the police called upon so quickly, the press would undoubtedly be involved too. They'd have a field day soon enough. But there was nothing to be done about it. Avi's unflinching decision to notify the police had been necessary in the face of the severity of what had happened. It was the first of the serendipitous, ingenuously correct steps in the denouement of events, given the baffling nature of what was to follow. But for now, none of us had a clue, except that everything had gone utterly topsy-turvy. And it was a very uneasy feeling indeed.

We moved off ramp. The wails gradually subsided, to be replaced by an even more unnerving silence. Though we were all together, this sudden, awful brush with mortality left each of us alone with our morbid dark thoughts.

I had no great love for Lajjo, she had been a veritable thorn in my side this entire training period in the contest. But I did respect her as a model, I understood and validated her extreme professionalism and her burning desire to win. I was the same way. And so, I was extremely sorry for her sudden and untimely demise. I harboured no ill will, nor that sense of subtle scheming, the kind those of lesser character might possess or secretly indulge in, now that the competition had been eliminated. My heart and head were clear of malice, that much was transparent, for all to see.

In fact, I was chagrined that it would now be an unequal contest. I suddenly wished her back fiercely, just so I could win fair and square. Illogical I know, but true all the same. But of course, that was not to be. My fervent wishing was childish and irrational, given the present grave circumstances. And clear evidence of the severe shock I was in at the time.

That time, and what followed that time was very hard to get through. We had all been witness to a gruesome death, macabre and surreal. But it wasn't until the police began with their investigation that sordid reality actually permeated our collective consciousness. That this was an out-and-out murder, not an inexplicable death, as I already knew it to be and it would be investigated as such—there was no getting around it.

The *Eye India* CEO, arriving out of breath and sweating, called for an urgent meeting with us, ostensibly to calm our delicate nerves, more plausibly to outline what must or must not be said in public.

But the police were having none of it. They wanted to speak to us all first, as a group, and then individually, starting with me of course—I was the one who had caught Lajjo as she fell. Also, I was the one who had an open, if forced rivalry with her at this contest. This was conveyed to Avi even before the police actually arrived at the venue. They swarmed all around in seconds, and when they did, there seemed so many of them. Most intimidating under the circumstances. The doctor and assorted medical professionals arrived minutes before them, confirming what we already knew—Lajjo was no more.

There were more shocks to follow. Naïve as we were, and deeply affected by what had happened to one of the brightest stars among us, we had not actually focused on the nature of the crime. And it was revealed to us that evening itself, in the form and voice of Additional Commissioner of Police, Crime, Dipankar Mhatre.

'You are all requested not to leave this room,' he told us, not wasting words as we gathered in the large hall of the hotel hosting the pageant, a little away from the stage we had been practising on, which was out in the adjoining open air auditorium.

We had no clue then how much attention this tragedy was being given by the powers that be. Now, in a different place, and so much older, I can say that few first-time transgressions generate the attention of the Addl.CP of the Crime Branch's personal involvement, that too with such immediacy.

We only knew that our sugar candy world had split at the seams. And this man before us, curt and business-like, and his equally grim faced constables, were all that stood between us and cruel reality. With his coming, we keenly sensed, I think, that dark and menacing intangibility that hovered, just over the periphery of our comprehension.

As we are ensconced in a world, a contest, driven primarily by appearance, let me describe Mhatre here. Browned by the sun, severe-looking, and of average height (which means most of the contestants towered above him, though not me) Mhatre looked to in his mid-thirties. Salt-and-pepper hair cut close, military style. Gaunt, all planes and angles his face, sharper seeming than it was because of the severity in his tone. We stared at him, silent as he continued.

'Given what we have learned, this is a murder that could have been committed by anyone.' He had a knack for understatement, spoke wonderfully good English, but there was only one person other than me who understood his words clearly. Understood the unsaid.

'He means we are *all suspects*,' Parvati's voice chimed out, bell-like and precise in that sepulchral atmosphere. There was a terrific sucking in of collective air, nobody knew quite what to do. There was no wailing or screaming or sobbing, even in protest this time—everybody was utterly spent, all cried out just a while before. There was no more shock left to express.

We were ostensibly such innocents; sheltered, protected, chaperoned everywhere by minders throughout the contest, our average ages not crossing twenty-three. It didn't occur to many of us, that despite the enormity of the crime and the public, audacious way it had been carried out, that we too had played a part in the gruesome narrative of Lajjo's demise. Having all been on stage when Lajjo walked her final walk— *we were all suspects now.*

There was more to this. Given the bizarre nature of this ghastly occurrence, there was also a distinct possibility that the contest itself might be cancelled. This, I think, was what was uppermost on our minds then, besides poor Lajjo's horrific demise. But with lightening quickness, the part about the cancellation was put to rest immediately by *Eye India.*

The pageant it seemed, was too big, too overreaching in both commercial and emotional aspects, not just in our minds and ambitions, but in the imagination of the country at large. How could there not be a Miss India contest that year?

No, calls had already been made at the highest levels— the *Eye India* organizers, grim-mannered and sombre, were obdurate. The show must go on. The police had to figure out the damage, nab the perpetrator, right this before it spun out of control. There was no other way.

Mhatre turned to Parvati, and her clear gaze met his levelly. 'Miss, please state your name. And then, if you could tell us exactly what happened, in your words, please?' Parvati's eyes held his. Steadfastly, she introduced herself, then began recounting all that had happened that morning.

Barely thirty minutes had passed between the macabre turn of events and the police's arrival on the premises, a remarkably quick response time. We were all in gowns of course, not the ones we would be wearing at the finale, but close enough so we could get our walks right. How could any of us have known as we dressed for this rehearsal what was to happen? That we would be seated here, nervy and tear spent in front of the inscrutable, saturnine Mr Mhatre before the day was out?

Listening to Parvati, voice firm, gaze straight, I couldn't help but feel a genuine stab of admiration. How composed she appeared, speaking so clearly, as if for us all, yet with respect for poor dead Lajjo. The reserved, if not ugly duckling, turned into a sanguine swan by devastating, unalterable circumstance. 'How did I not notice you before, Ms Samant?' I thought to myself. 'You are a person worth getting to know ...'

Addl.CP Mhatre was just getting started. It was initially conveyed to Avi that the police would want to speak to me first. But Parvati's out of turn outburst had tweaked the proceedings. Once she was done, he requested we speak to him individually. His men were already vetting the scene of crime. The blade, as murder weapon, had been sealed, on its way to Forensics by now, to be dusted for fingerprints. Record time for an investigation of this nature, but we didn't know that then either.

Mhatre went into a corner room, adjacent to the hall we were congregated in. We were to go in one by one to narrate our version of that morning. And answer any other questions the Addl.CP might choose to ask.

'I want to get it over with,' stated Myra, the girl who had lost control at the sight of Lajjo's blood earlier on. Even though the police had specifically asked for me to go in, she wanted to be first so she could go lie down. The police officer asked for her name, for the record. To us, meanwhile, Myra didn't have a last name. Here's why.

Though we were all winners of regional contests, or representatives of the smaller states, once we were at this level i.e. the national competition, we dropped our regional titles. It was deemed politically incorrect that year to highlight our regional origins, even our religion for that matter.

There was a grim reason for this, and it had to do with events beyond the cossetted reality of our contest. This was the 1995 pageant, barely a couple of years post the 1992-early 1993 Mumbai communal riots. The resulting army lockdown over the city, followed by the March 1993 bomb blasts were still fresh in people's minds circa 1995. As a safeguard, even in a beauty contest with no evident political agenda, the CEO of *Eye India* that year had decreed that the contestants be known only by their first names. Nothing would give away what religion we practised, not even the region we represented. Thus the sashes we would wear through-out the contest as identification for judges marking us, only revealed our birth name—no surname. And our contest number, naturally.

Recounting what happened, I find it necessary now to give certain full names—of those who were anyway established on the fashion circuit, like Lajjo or Avi or I, or those who mattered to the story, like Addl.CP Mhatre, or simply those I got to know better, like Parvati.

Also, in 1995, India had fewer states than it does now. At the regional-level pre-contests, some states and union territories had been clubbed together into areas, with an overall winner selected. So despite the actual number of states and territories, the total number of contestants on this, the national stage stood at twenty-one and now an even twenty without Lajjo. Twenty bewildered beauty contest hopefuls, each wishing this nightmare wasn't real.

Myra was granted leave to speak first. The rest of the girls, silent till now, burst into nervous twitter once the Addl.CP vacated the hall and she shut the door behind her, following him and his small unit in.

'My God, what'll happen now?' one of the gathered contestants, Samantha, tittered. Breathless seeming, because she spoke all in a rush.

'Everyone's doing what is necessary,' Parvati's dry tone in sharp contrast to Samantha's, lowered the intensity in the room a notch. 'We just need to tell them all we know.'

'But they're saying we're *all* suspects,' Anuradha, a fair girl with really long hair chimed in worriedly.

'They think one of us *killed* Lajjo!' Nina, one of the girls who had fainted earlier, whispered. 'Why would we? Who could think of doing such a thing?' She looked at each of us in turn, her eyes suddenly fearful as the true import of what she had just uttered hit her. 'They're saying they think one of us could be a *murderer* ...'

3

Akruti

⌣

Before long, Myra was out. Our nerves were so strained we didn't know if she was questioned by the police for a long time or not. It was my turn to meet the dour Mr Mhatre.

'Ms Rai,' he addressed me as I stepped into the room. It must have been a mini conference room of some sort, either that or he had requested the hotel to add the table and chairs that were now facing me. Addl.CP Mhatre gestured to me to sit down. He sat behind the table, his officers behind him, like a wall. They had seemed so many when they arrived, but now, in the room itself, there were four, apart from Mhatre. The rest had obviously fanned out on the premises, possibly collecting statements or evidence.

I sat where he indicated. He didn't ask for my name, as he had of Parvati earlier. Obviously, given my celebrity status, it wasn't necessary. 'You knew the victim well?' was his first question.

'Lajjo used to model with me, so I suppose I knew her longer than the others,' I acquiesced. 'Better? I don't know. We were the only two professional models in this contest, but we weren't friendly.'

'She was your rival, professionally, I take it,' Mhatre probed. I was wrung out by all that had occurred, though the

31

time lapse between occurrence and interrogation hadn't been long drawn out at all. But I knew I had to keep my head, not break down and babble, out of stupid panic, or shock, or just abject emotional fatigue.

'Professionally? I don't think so. As you know, though I am a Mumbai girl, I'm well established in fashion circles,' I said more coolly than I felt. For good measure, I smiled a cursory half-smile at his team. In the few and far between moments I had interacted with police people—at a traffic signal, at a parking space—I had always got a gratifying response at flashing my smile. Most knew me from television or ads and were vocal in expressing admiration, all else aside.

But Mhatre and his team remained unimpressed with my effort to charm them, this I realised straightaway. Their faces stayed inscrutable. The Crime Branch, as is the sobering nature of their job, tend to ignore surface appearances. Or at least, this team did. Who I was didn't matter. What I might have done most certainly did.

I decided to be as honest as I possibly could, with all the forthrightness of my character that had served me well thus far. 'Addl.CP Mhatre? If you're asking me whether I disliked Lajjo, the answer is no. I didn't know her well enough. She wasn't as successful as me, you know that already, I'm sure. If you're asking whether I was afraid she would win the crown over me, I'd say sure, as any contestant would be. A healthy anxiety, because she was beautiful and confident and had experience catwalking in front of actual audiences, unlike the rest. If you're asking whether I have reason to hate her or hurt her for that, the answer is no, because it isn't something a sane person, which I definitely am, would think of doing. I happen to believe competition, especially from a worthy rival, makes any victory sweeter. I have great faith in my own abilities, and you will know, from my career so far, this has served me well. So if you're asking if I killed her, the answer, Addl.CP Mhatre is absolutely not.'

For the first time in this awful day, I saw a glimmer of what looked like the ghost of a smile appear on Mhatre's face, but it was replaced almost instantly by the familiar stony appearance.

'Where were you exactly? Can you draw a map for me, please? And describe precisely what you saw. Take your time, give me any detail, anything you felt was different or amiss as well.'

But after my monologue, I sensed there was a subtle change in the atmosphere in the room. This astute team of sleuths had made a judgement call, no doubt based on their extensive experience. They said nothing, showed nothing. But long hours of working with the hyper-perceptive Avi had taught me a little about picking up nuances, recognizing the hidden in the unsaid. I understood there and then, that somehow, though it wasn't ever voiced or even evident in any tangible manner—I was not really a strong suspect in their minds.

'I had just finished posing at the top of the ramp, in fashion terminology it is called head ramp,' I began, taking his pencil and drawing a rough sketch of all our positions as I spoke. 'I was waiting for Lajjo to join me. The rest of the girls were on either side of ramp, also waiting. Lajjo was at base ramp and walking towards me.'

'Was there anything unusual in that?' Mhatre asked.

'No, it was all part of the finale sequence, as Avi had choreographed it. But ...' I paused. 'I noticed two things.' I had suddenly remembered my surprise at Lajjo's behaviour. 'Lajjo had started walking towards me before the music began.

Her cue was the music starting, she had never pre-empted it before. None of us overstep Avi's choreography. He has a temper, demands perfection. And Lajjo was too much of a professional to defy him at any point. I remember thinking it was strange she had started walking so early. In fact, when Avi called the cue over the mic, she was already at midpoint on ramp. She never made mistakes, unless she did it on purpose this time.'

'I see,' Mhatre was looking at me intently. 'And do you think there might have been a reason for her commencing early?'

I drew a deep breath. Better to come clean here, better he heard it from me than others. No doubt he would be told, anyway. 'I had not entered the sequence from where I was supposed to,' I addressed him. 'I was experimenting. As Avi had too, by changing the track abruptly just today, for that very scene. I was to enter from the wings after Lajjo, as at every rehearsal. But I didn't—I entered from the audience, using the stairs connecting the front seating to ramp. It was unplanned, I did it on the spur of the moment, on whim. Perhaps Lajjo might have felt pressured to up her game too? Maybe she started earlier than her cue thinking she too would experiment? But there was a difference—I had already alerted Avi just seconds before I entered, asked him to watch me as I changed the flow of his choreography. Lajjo took the decision without his knowledge. She isn't as senior in the fraternity as I am, and the finale was a vital sequence. I knew then, I'm sure the others did too, that it would not be taken well. Besides, something tells me there's more to it. She was not an impulsive person, and she always wanted to please Avi. This was not the way, we all knew it. It was a strange thing to do.'

Mhatre's eyes told me that he was paying very close attention. So was his team.

'You said there was a second thing?' He continued.

'Yes,' I said. 'Lajjo is very graceful on stage. But there was a moment this time that she faltered in her walk. I was at a distance, way up the long ramp, but I still saw her stumble. Could've been nothing, it happens to the best of us. But Lajjo had never ever tripped during rehearsal before.'

'When was this?' Mhatre wanted to know. 'And could you also write down the names of all the girls and where exactly each one was standing, please? Also, where exactly did she stumble? Who was standing next to her when she did?'

'We've been practising so long I could give you each girl's placement in a heartbeat. But I cannot tell you exactly where Lajjo stumbled,' I told him. 'The lights had dimmed by then, we only saw Lajjo. She was in the spot, you see. And when that happens, you tend to see only the person the spot is on, even if the others aren't always hidden on the sides.'

'Did she stumble again, or only once?' Mhatre persisted.

'I saw it happen once, roughly as she neared midpoint of ramp,' I said. 'After that, after she reached midway, the choreography changed for me. I had to turn to face the audience rather than the stage and the girls on ramp. With my back to them, I had to wait for Lajjo to reach me; sense her rather than see her. So I couldn't tell if she stumbled again, because I didn't see. But yes, her steps were not the same as at every rehearsal. I did notice that.' I added sombrely.

Suddenly I remembered the lone red light, blinking as I waited for Lajjo to join me.

'But the camera would tell you all this better,' I told Mhatre. He leaped at the opening, as I had known he would.

'What camera?' he asked sharply. A low buzz was suddenly audible among his team as well, so far silent. No one had bothered to inform them about the lone camera recording the rehearsal.

I enlightened him and he immediately, curtly, requested two men to go secure the recordings.

'When did she fall?' Mhatre continued, laser-attentive, after his men had left to search for the camera. Maybe he realized then, that my powers of observation and of retention were not ordinary. Avi, as star choreographer, was familiar with this ability of mine, used to reserve the most complicated ramp sequences for me alone, knowing I would come through, and magnificently so. Addl.CP Mhatre was just waking up to the fact that the fashion celebrity in front of him had more to her credit and character than mere outward appearances.

'When I turned to face her,' I said, utterly weary now, but determined to appear otherwise. I would not show my mind numbing exhaustion to this impassive stranger, my pride would not allow for it. 'According to Avi's choreography we both had to do a double turn—she, as she approached from stage, and me turning from the audience. Upon finishing, we would end up standing shoulder to shoulder facing the audience and begin peeling off on opposite sides of ramp for the final bow, all the others following us. She was to pirouette with me, but when I turned, I found her standing still, facing me. Her expression was vacant, as if she wasn't really present. The front of her gown looked damp, I thought she was sweating under the lights. Then she toppled onto me, and I caught her. And I realized it was actually blood, the gown's wine colour masking the red ...'

'Everyone saw this?' Mhatre asked.

'We were in the spot. Everyone could,' I replied. 'Everyone watching could see me I know, including the camera. There was no way I could've thrust the blade into Lajjo from behind, even if anyone feels so. She was already falling from the blow when she got to me. I caught her as her life slipped away, I know this ...'

The officer locked eyes with me, he understood how tired I was now.

'You have been an observant witness,' he said gently. 'But your enmity, real or imagined, is documented, mentioned to us by a few we spoke to earlier, here. She fell into your arms. The camera will tell us more, but we have to obtain the recording first. I want to know—will you be hiring a lawyer now, Ms Rai?'

People say I have always been peculiar in that my instinct is never wrong. It has helped me through a number of sticky situations and I have always abided by it. My instinct today told me there was a lot going against me. Especially should some ill-willed type, decide to malign me, as I had, no doubt, in the course of my blitzkrieg career, made as many jealous enemies as supportive friends. Also, I was publically thought to be Lajjo's rival in this contest, and our fates were inextricably linked in that she had died in my arms.

I had never been in any situation like this before. In the hindsight of age and wisdom, it occurs to me, the first thing I ought to have considered then, was to protect myself legally. But I was younger at the time, flush with the naiveté of the foolish or the brave. Not knowing otherwise, I believed that my innocence would keep me safe.

The police could no doubt make my life difficult, should they choose to. But to what avail? The men in this room were seasoned, I felt their experience gave them foresight in their work. They didn't believe I killed Lajjo, I could see it in their eyes. And despite his taciturn nature, Addl.CP Mhatre seemed both sensible and competent at his job.

'I don't think I need one yet, Addl.CP Mhatre,' I said, with deep sincerity, willing him to understand that I trusted the process and his team so far. Trusted them to gauge my innocence.

If I had expected surprise at my fool-hardiness in refusing to hire some sort of safeguard to protect myself, there was none. Mhatre appeared to reserved judgement. Or he was trained not to show it.

'I see,' he said. 'Now, if you would complete that drawing for me, please? Also, we're finished at present, but don't go too far. I would like to have you tell me a bit more about each contestant, if you can, a little later. And we would be asking this of everyone, once the initial questioning is complete. I'm not asking right now because I'm hoping the camera recording you've mentioned will answer some questions first. We'll take it from there.'

I handed him the drawing of our positions on the ramp, with each girl's name on it. I let myself out the door, checking my watch for the first time since rehearsal had started. It was nearing 8 p.m. and the police had barely begun their investigation. It was going to be a very long day indeed.

As I entered the waiting hall again, I saw the policemen Mhatre had sent to fetch the camera hurrying back with it from the amphitheatre—clearly they had found the piece and would now watch the entire rehearsal themselves. Thus gaining real-time, blow by blow knowledge of the unfurling of events.

Quite possibly they might also get a glimpse of how Lajjo had been attacked, perhaps even her attacker. It depended on the camera angle—this one was not a mobile unit, nor was anyone operating it remotely, so it only captured the ramp and centre stage. It had a simple function, to be recording the sequence from straight up ahead of us, facing ramp, facing *us,* so we would not be intimidated by all those cameras pointed at us from exactly that position on the final day.

But there was a fine chance that it might just have managed to capture something important, even so. Exhausted as I was, I was intrigued at the thought that the police might find a way to end this horror story that night itself—if they happened to actually *spot* Lajjo's attacker on film.

The next girl, Samantha, I think it was, left to go in to meet the Addl.CP once I came into the waiting room. There was a hush in the hall now, the intense strain of the past few hours was beginning to show on everyone. We were all emotionally weary, our nerves shot. I think the girls wanted to just get away, go rest, process that day's miserable turn of events in solitude. But that wasn't possible yet. So they sat around in wait for their turn, listless, contemplative, or coalesced in small groups talking in low voices. The atmosphere was decidedly funereal.

As I waited, went over what the camera might have recorded. in my mind. I ran over the faces of the girls edging the ramp in my minds-eye, trying to decide where exactly it was that I saw Lajjo falter.

She may have been the only one in spot, the rest of us invisible to the audience or even the camera perhaps, but we knew everyone's placement like the back of our hands. Was it as she passed Pia? Nisha? Wait a minute … my brow furrowed in puzzlement, I suddenly recalled a face at the edge of ramp, shaded by the spot's forced darkness (was it one of the girls?), that shouldn't have been there. But why not?

I couldn't quite get to it, what was it in that remembered scene that had so disturbed my memory? Weariness and emotions were making my memory hazy, but it was there, the reason for my uneasiness. It was right below the surface--the abstract sense of something not quite right about the formation. What was I missing? Maybe Avi would know. I decided I would ask him as soon as I saw him.

'Did it go okay?' Parvati's voice interrupted my thoughts, I looked up to find her eyes on me, an unobtrusive but kind empathy evident.

'Yes, I think so. They even asked me if I was getting legal representation. But I don't think I will be,' I said to her.

Parvati opened her mouth to say something but Helen, coming up close right then, pulled at her to ask her something. As Parvati turned, distracted, the memory hit me sharply, followed immediately by an awful foreboding.

Parvati—it was Parvati's face I had seen in shadow as Lajjo stumbled … not close to her, no, but in the wrong place, five girls too far from her actual place on ramp. She should've been standing at midpoint, fairly near the place where Lajjo had tripped. But she hadn't been … she wasn't where she should've been … *why?*

As realization at the interchange dawned, my gaze met Parvati's, standing in front of me again, now free of Helen's intervention. It must've shown in my eyes, my sudden wariness, for Parvati it appeared was also adept at reading nuance. Just as clearly as Avi, maybe more so, I later realized.

In an instant, she had come up close, so close I could smell the mint on her breath, see the fine crinkly lines under her eyes courtesy the stage make-up. Caked and creasing now, much too dry after a relentless day. 'Not here,' she whispered, the urgency hard and brittle in her voice. '*Come with me …*'

4

Akruti

Parvati took my arm firmly, dragging my not-entirely-unprotesting figure to a far corner of the room, as discreetly as she could manage without appearing to be in a panic. She had the advantage of height of course, but we were evenly matched for strength should things get out of hand. In fact she was thinner than I was, lighter too, I was certain in that split second that I would be able to bring her down if she tried anything funny. But all she wanted to do was talk to me.

'Akruti, you need to listen to me first, without interrupting, please,' she spoke in a low tone, her resolute eyes boring into mine, *willing* me to acquiesce. I jerked my arm away from her hold, rubbing the sore spot where it had contacted the insistent strength of her fingers.

'I don't need to do anything,' my tone was edged with the icy hauteur perfected over years dealing with assertive production in-charges, though I was doing her the courtesy of keeping my voice low. 'I don't like being pulled around or pressured.'

I would've continued in this manner, but something in her eyes silenced me. My unerring instinct took over, and I bowed to its wisdom instantly.

'Tell me,' I capitulated, curt, all arrogance dissolved.

She understood the shift in the mood, and rose to greet it without preamble.

'I wasn't where I was supposed to be on ramp, when Lajjo walked that last walk,' she said. 'I know you know. But Akruti—*I didn't kill her*. I couldn't have, I was too far away in the formation, you know this too. Besides, I had no reason to.'

I watched Parvati. Her eyes, serious and intense, did not seem to be those of a murderer. But then, I hadn't met too many murderers, so how would I know, really?

'I'll have to tell the police,' I told her, still brusque. 'They will need to know that the formation was skewed on ramp when Lajjo walked that walk.'

'Yes,' Parvati was still maintaining eye contact, her gaze troubled, but her eyes clear. 'You should. I will tell them myself, when I am called in. But you understand why I dragged you away just now, right? I didn't want you creating a commotion, letting it be known the ramp formation was not correct. Because, Akruti—whether or not you believe I killed Lajjo, I *know* I didn't. It is possible that only you and I realise that the formation was awry, at present. Everyone appears to be too confused. Your yelling just now would've alerted them all, even those who weren't aware … including the *real* killer …'

'I wouldn't have yelled,' I told Parvati coldly. 'You don't know me, so I won't push the point. But I do agree with you. It does make sense that only the police know the formation was different this rehearsal. If anyone else hits upon it, they would've spoken up or spoken to the police. Better for the investigation, this silence. And safer for us, I guess,' I voiced what she had left unsaid. That if whoever had murdered Lajjo understood we were thinking hard about the circumstances surrounding that last walk rather than just ourselves, realized we knew the formation was skewed, they might also fear we'd uncover their identity soon enough. And get to *us*, before the police intervened.

'Let's start over,' Parvati's voice was cool, in response to my tone, but I picked up on the peace offering nuance. 'You and I—*we* were there, the police weren't. This affects everything, and I still want the contest to end in a positive space, despite everything. Besides, Lajjo didn't deserve this—we should help find the culprit the best we can.'

I met her earnest gaze. The sincerity in her tone had appealed to my forthright nature immediately. I recalled her previous composure while dealing with Mhatre, the calmness and efficiency even earlier at the ramp itself—her willingness to step forward to help me first, when all the rest were frozen, stiff with shock.

'You are right, Parvati,' I said, all hauteur dropping from my voice. 'Lajjo didn't deserve this. I want to help any way I can. So, let's figure this out, think, match notes. If we hit upon something we need to let the Addl.CP know. Because I too want this contest to finish better than this ...'

In hindsight, I think this was the exact moment when our pact of mutual support was born, though we didn't know it then.

'We need to reason on two levels,' Parvati went on. 'The first—what exactly was the formation when Lajjo walked? Besides me, who else was not in their place? Were they close to her?' She produced a diary and started jotting down points with a pen as she spoke.

I always knew Parvati to be quiet, even bookish, but this diary business went a step beyond.

'You're writing this down?' I asked, incredulous.

'And the second ... difficult as it is to process, let's think about each of us—as a *murderer*,' Parvati ignored my outburst and got to the heart of the matter at hand. '*Who among us would want Lajjo dead?*'

'You mean apart from the obvious suspect—*me*?' Clearly the strain of the day had crept up unannounced. My out-of-character retort, with its dark, unsuited humour wasn't taken to at all. In fact, Parvati ignored my comment, as if she hadn't heard it.

'We need to think of all the contestants, their relation to Lajjo, friendships, enmities, who we know them to be. Writing it all down will help.' She said.

I knew this was logical, and there was a sincerity to her efforts. But my instinct was not to cooperate. At nineteen, it is a rare personality who will go about trying to help the police and solve a horrible, emotionally exhausting crime in such an organised manner.

True, Parvati's very personality was efficient and orderly. And yet, this documentation, this meticulous and precise approach—it seemed much too practised. Almost as if she knew how to go about an investigation. How could she, though? So there were two things that needed my immediate attention.

'Let's outline each of the girls' positions, also adding what we think of them, and their relation to Lajjo,' I concurred, holding my hand out to Parvati in a simple gesture of camaraderie.

That was the first thing—compiling a list of suspects. The second one had to be done on my own. I made a mental note to get on it, as soon as this awful day ended and I had some me-time. It would hold till then, but only just.

'Let's get started,' Parvati replied, shaking my outstretched hand cursorily, then re ordering the pages in her diary. 'We don't have much time.'

'Myra?' I said. 'Shall we start with her?'

'Myra,' Parvati murmured, writing the name down in her notebook. 'Let's discuss each, I'll write down what we think as we do.'

'She stood the closest to me on ramp,' I began. 'At the edge of head ramp, in fact, very far from Lajjo. And hadn't moved, not since I began my climb via the stairs to ramp from up front. I saw her as I made my entry from stage, was conscious of her there all along, being closest to me. Just behind her, on the other side of the ramp, was Helen. She too didn't move, nor changed position.'

The formation was such that the girls were interspersed, one behind the other who was standing on the *opposite* side of ramp, the continuous diamond formation and gaps necessary so everyone could be seen by the audience.

'Myra appeared very nervy—so nervy she requested to go first to the police, even before you,' Parvati said. 'That could be a point to keep in mind. She may not have actually felt what she so convincingly put on … panic.'

'Perhaps,' my eyebrows had furrowed in concentration. 'But what motive could she possibly have to kill Lajjo? She wasn't a front runner even in the sub-contests. And her fear appeared genuine. In fact, being closest to me in the formation, she was the first to spot the blood flowing from Lajjo as I held her body; no wonder Myra was the first to start screaming. Also, she did not change position at all, remember?'

'Strike Myra's name, then,' Parvati mumbled, cap in her mouth as she whisked it off the pen and struck Myra off her suspect list. Till now we weren't really conscious as to our own actions, but as we put pen to paper in this methodical fashion, it hit us—we were actually *investigating* a fellow contestant's murder, albeit in a rudimentary manner.

'Helen, ditto,' Parvati continued. 'No reason to kill Lajjo, not a front runner in sub-contests nor a media favorite. Plus she didn't move from her position at all.'

Without saying it, we were both relieved, I think. Helen was one of the nicer girls at the pageant, a desi with an NRI accent, having been schooled all over the world. Her father was a diplomat and she, with her little-girl-lost sweetness and intrinsic charm, had managed to befriend most of the other contestants. For all her sweetness though, Helen lacked ambition, I felt. 'We'll move the discussion one girl at a time, front of ramp to back,' Parvati murmered. 'So far there's Myra, Helen ... you.'

'I was near the audience seating the whole time,' I spoke softly. It shouldn't matter what Parvati thought really, it was the police who were most important. But if we were doing this even in a small way, better to do it right. 'I was visible at all times, and always up front, not in the wings. I even approached ramp from the front.'

'You did,' Parvati looked up to meet my eyes for a fraction, before dropping her gaze back to the diary. 'It's more than possible she was stabbed *before* she reached you, she was walking so funny when she passed me.'

'Glad for the vote of confidence,' I said, a trifle wryly. 'The police will rule out nothing yet though, because she fell into my arms.'

'I can understand their reasoning,' Parvati said. 'So could you, if you think unemotionally, as if it were not you but another person in exactly your place. Because it's just too pat—beautiful model stumbling a few paces, then falling into the arms of a contestant who just happens to be her arch-rival in the contest … only to die immediately after, like in a luridly written novel. Unreal.'

'That's just it, Parvati,' I said. 'This whole thing, from the word go, has had this air of unreality. "Staged" may not be the appropriate word, but just artificial, you know. Somehow, appearing *created*.'

'How odd you say that,' Parvati looked at me. 'I thought the same thing. Could it be because it was … how can I put this—*pre*-planned? It was supposed to happen, only *differently* than it did today, because something was different, *became* different, because it happened out of the blue? Like our formation, for instance, which had me in a different place and two or three other girls as well … we hadn't rehearsed it, or planned it, it was circumstance. But it could've changed a well laid plan most drastically.'

'You mean perhaps someone *plotted* for days or weeks or months to stab Lajjo like this,' my voice was hushed as I first took in what Parvati was saying and then realized it could be no other way. This was no crime of passion, sudden anger or temper resulting in grievous consequence. Not up on ramp like this—it was most certainly premeditated, carefully carried out in a cold-blooded kind of way, audacious, public and final.

'So most elementarily, it comes down to motive,' Parvati's half-smiled, but the attempt at humour did little to lighten to mood. We were too worn out.

'You said circumstance'. I spoke up. 'You and two-three girls were not in formation because of circumstance—what does that mean?'

Parvati's eyes held mine. 'Smriti and Vanessa wanted to go pee,' she said. 'They went to the restroom during the blackout.'

I could not believe my ears. We had been warned not to shift position during the thirty second blackout, because the television cameras would record all. Dark moving shapes are visible in a blackout and a camera's recording can show these up clearer than if one was seated, watching from a live audience.

But today, four days to D-Day, rehearsals had been gruelling, some of us had not even managed a bathroom break, forget snack break, so intent were we on getting everything perfect. No wonder it had come to this—a sneaky exit in blackout time, the urge uncontrollable, even at the risk of igniting Avi's thunderous temper if found out.

'When you gotta go, you gotta go,' Parvati said, a trifle ruefully, the laugh lines round her mouth deepening despite the present morbidity. 'They ran back as soon as they could, but couldn't reach their places in time. So we all shifted, both lines on either side, to compensate, right up to where Samantha and I were standing on the other side.'

I was close to speechless. What does one say when something so silly, yet so absolutely unimaginable occurs?

'Myra, Helen opposite her, then Nuzhat behind Helen on Myra's side, and Anuradha behind Nuzhat—they all seemed to be in their correct place,' I mused, concentrating very hard now. 'All of them were at the very front of ramp clearly visible as I walked up the stairs to the ramp.'

'Yes.' Parvati's tone was patient. 'The formation changed only upto Samantha, opposite to Anuradha, just behind her. The entire block basically moved two girls down, one place on each side actually, to accommodate Smriti and Vanessa's frantic presence at base of ramp, returning from their restroom break. They were unable to reach beyond that point before the blackout ended.'

'So that means a number of girls were in incorrect positions, not just two or three,' I said worriedly. 'I could only see upto Nisha and Pia when the spot came on, not behind them, didn't realize immediately that so much had changed ...'

'It'll be easier if we drew this out.' I told Parvati.

Parvati showed me a page of her diary. Already drawn out, meticulous and neat—each girl's position at the time Lajjo walked her final walk.

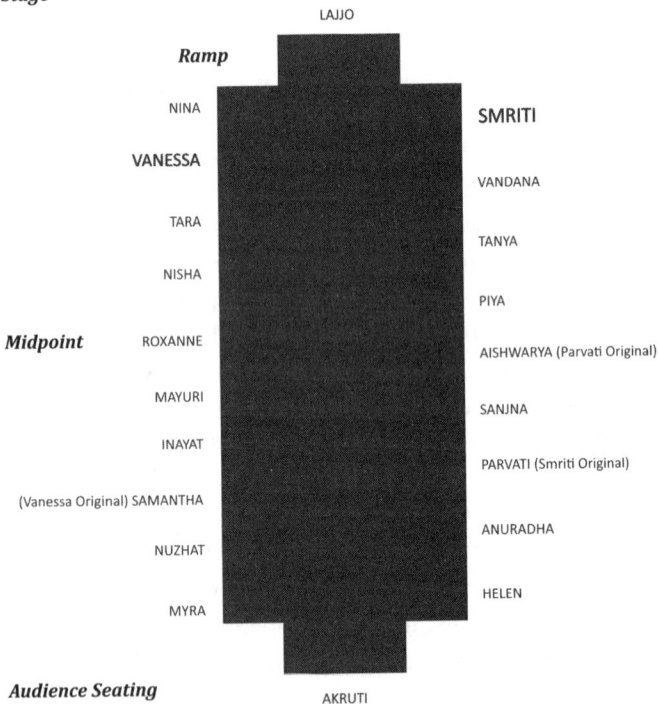

Stage

Ramp

LAJJO

NINA

SMRITI

VANESSA

VANDANA

TARA

TANYA

NISHA

PIYA

Midpoint   ROXANNE

AISHWARYA (Parvati Original)

MAYURI

SANJNA

INAYAT

PARVATI (Smriti Original)

(Vanessa Original) SAMANTHA

ANURADHA

NUZHAT

HELEN

MYRA

Audience Seating

AKRUTI

I scrutinized the drawing, unsurprised at Parvati's efficiency and accuracy of line placement. I was beginning to catch on to just how particular she could be.

'Sanjna,' I said. 'She doesn't appear to be standing where she was supposed to, especially if everyone only moved two girls below. One girl below, actually, because each was on the opposite side of ramp ... wasn't she *after* you in the original formation? You were to be at midpoint or just after as the original formation, in this, you're almost five girls down, counting both sides.'

'We'll need to note down every girl's position on this map, and mark out the ones we aren't sure of.' Parvati nodded. 'Sanjna *was* after me in formation. But on the rehearsal day, she stood before me. When I came back to ramp, she was already in position, in fact.'

'When you *came back to ramp*?' But we were all to hold position during the blackout. Are you saying, that you too were on a restroom break at this time?' I was incredulous, my nerves fraught by the rate of on-going revelations. 'And you actually managed to get back to position despite that?'

'I am saying that I wasn't on ramp. I did manage to reach close to my position just before the lights came on,' Parvati said softly. 'But I wasn't on a restroom break. I was stiff, needed just a second to stretch.'

I met her eyes, unshadowed and guileless. No matter what she said or how innocent she looked saying it, things just didn't add up. We had been rehearsing the same sequence for ages. Today had been a long day and maybe restroom breaks were justified. But breaks to stretch out stiff limbs? How was this the one rehearsal when so many of Avi's instructions were ignored?

I wanted to trust her, this cool, tall girl who seemed to know so much and was so self-assured in all she did. But so much about her was unexplained. Her intentions seemed genuine, as did her will to try and get to the bottom of this awfulness we found ourselves in. But I had questions and it looked as if I would need more time to get answers for them from her.

'Parvati, you are an enigma, perhaps as much as this mysterious darkness we find ourselves embroiled in,' I thought, watching her as she scribbled on in her diary. 'But I won't settle, Ms Samant. I *will* find out about you, even if there's stuff you don't want to reveal for the moment.'

Parvati could keep her secrets. I had an ace up my sleeve and I believed it was time I used it. This was the 'second thing' that I had mentioned earlier, the one I had to get to. Not an 'it' actually. More like a 'him'.

5

Akruti

⌒

'Shall we continue?' Parvati moved her pen briskly down her drawing, impatient at my sudden silence. 'Inayat, Mayuri, Aishwarya, Roxanne—they had all moved one girl up, but hadn't left the stage.'

'I see,' I said. 'The only person who had moved two girls up, and four-five girls up if you count both sides of ramp, would be you, Parvati.'

'Yes, that's true,' Parvati said. 'Not that it means much. Had I stayed in formation, I would've been almost at midpoint.'

'The point Lajjo stumbled at, or close to it,' I pointed out. 'I saw her.'

'Did you?' Parvati's eyes narrowed as she looked at me, gaze alert, inquiring. 'We were all turned slightly outwards, facing the audience, even if the formation was skewed. And Lajjo was in spot, all else dark or just about. You actually were in a fortuitous position, Akruti, right at the very top of ramp, facing us. Because you could see everything—almost like a camera. It is fantastic, how observant you are!'

'Yes, maybe,' I said, suddenly bone-weary. 'But somehow, nothing unusual comes to mind, other than your change in position. I've been trying to go over what I saw till I turned to face the audience, but I cannot recall anything amiss. Just

Lajjo's stumble mid-ramp or so. Then the fact that she started walking before Avi's cue.'

'She did?' Parvati looked incredulous. 'Why?' Watching her amazement it occurred to me that there was actually *no way* Lajjo would have walked in defiance of Avi. Though I had mentioned to Addl.CP Mhatre that it might've been ego on Lajjo's part, it was just not possible, I now realised. She had clearly not been herself. But why? Or rather—how?

'She was stabbed *before* she walked the entire ramp,' Parvati answered her own question with sudden conviction, reiterating her earlier surmise to me. 'She was already losing blood, though it was camouflaged by her red gown. It is possible *no one* on ramp put the blade in ...'

'It is,' I agreed, watching her carefully, thinking ... 'Or they did when they left during blackout. But, Parvati—why did Lajjo not call or cry out when stabbed? And how could she continue to walk the entire length of the ramp if she was stabbed *before*? Even if she was dazed from the stabbing and that's what messed up the timing of her walk. We need to think that through. Regardless, from what you say, two girls left the stage, which never happened before in rehearsal blackout. And, Parvati? You did too.'

'Yes,' Parvati's face was impassive as she continued her reconstruction of the events. 'Pia, Nisha, Tania, Tara Vandana—all of them were at the very back, shifted to accommodate Vanessa and Smriti coming in. The girl who stayed put almost at base stage right at the back of ramp was Nina—she retained her position all through, even when the girls returned. I don't think anyone else moved off stage apart from the three of us, though positions shifted for many. We should double-check that, though.'

'I don't know how I didn't see so much movement,' I said, a trifle bitterly. 'I was facing stage in the blackout. But I was thinking only of myself, concentrating on my pose. I was picturing the audience watching my back. I was showing it off, all my attention was on *me* ...'

'Understandable,' said Parvati almost gently. 'You weren't to know. But *now*, you must try and recall, use all your powers of retention.'

I nodded. 'There is also the camera,' I added. 'The one at head ramp. Even if the girls want to hide their movements for some reason, it would show who held position and who didn't.'

'Maybe we should get our hands on that recording first,' Parvati said. 'We'd be faster at arriving at our suspects.'

'It's already with the police,' I said. 'I saw them going with the camera to the room where the Addl.CP is, earlier. Why would they let us see it at all?'

'Why, indeed,' said Parvati grimly. 'It's evidence now. But they might be willing to make their own jobs easier. We could save them the effort of piecing together who was standing where and trying to figure out diagrams and drawings on cue sheets. We could be in the room while they watch it, helping them. It's worth a try, don't you think?'

Parvati was already zipping up her diary in her bag, her brisk efficiency in sharp contrast to our wan mood. I followed her wordlessly back to the room where the Addl.CP was grilling the contestants. It was already almost 9 p.m. Nearing dinner, but who was hungry, really?

Parvati knocked on the door of the mini conference room. She stepped in boldly. I followed.

Addl.CP Mhatre looked up, he had just finished with one of the girls and was in discussion with his team before summoning the next.

'We'd like to help you when you watch the recording of the rehearsal,' Parvati said, wasting no words. 'We would be able to tell you who exactly was where, especially if people had moved around.'

There was silence in the room. The Addl.CP looked at us for a long while. He seemed to make up his mind.

'We've already watched it,' he said curtly. 'But it would save time if you told us who was where as the camera runs. We'll play it again. Take a seat.'

I couldn't believe how easy that had been. I was expecting a cool rejection, followed by a speedy dismissal from the room. But here we were, seated with the Addl.CP and team, about to watch a live grab of our finale gown sequence rehearsal ... and Lajjo's final moments. I suddenly felt a bit nauseous. We hadn't eaten much and to go through watching Lajjo collapse all over again might not be such a great idea after all.

'Not a time to be squeamish,' Parvati's sharp words in my ear gave me a jolt. 'If we have to get to the bottom of this, we need to watch this without nerves.'

Her words provided the much needed succour, enough for me to regain composure.

'I'm ready,' I whispered back. The recording began. I watched myself go up the ramp from the front, pose, as Lajjo, feisty and still in her element retreated to base ramp as I took her place. The music roared to a crescendo, then faded. Lights out, spot cut, as per Avi's cue. The thirty-second blackout came on. The camera stayed focused, every shape visible, half-lit in the dark haze, but distinct. As we watched, two shapes nearer the top of the ramp, their placement closer to the camera, detached themselves from the formation and silently moved towards the back entrance.

'Smriti and Vanessa,' Parvati turned to the Addl.CP, even as another shape, standing closer to mid-ramp, followed the previous two off the ramp.

'And that would be me,' Parvati added, her voice absolutely steadfast. The Addl.CP made no comment, the recording was still running. The camera, positioned dead-centre, head ramp, could capture the first few girls right on top of ramp, perhaps to mid-point. The ones behind, even though visible, were indistinct in the haze.

The tape continued, we saw the silent shuffling as the girls who had left took different places and Parvati rejoined the formation, but in a different place. The sequence began once again. We saw Lajjo walk, pre-empting the music, still in darkness, a trifle unsteady. We watched the stage lights come on, to Avi's cue. Lajjo in spot, already too far ahead of the music, catwalking to join me. Watching it as observer, her slow sashay seemed laborious to me. *She must already have been losing blood, and none of us knew ...* I watched myself make the turn to face the audience, feeling quite ill now, in anticipation of what would follow. The Addl.CP stopped the recording at this point.

'The rest is not relevant.' he said. We understood he was sparing us having to relive those moments again. And we knew there was nothing more that happened then, Lajjo had already been stabbed earlier, bleeding as she walked. Watching the recording had convinced us of this.

'We will try to zoom in on the formation in the recording step by step to see if the girls at the back also moved or left the stage.' The Addl.CP said. 'We might need you to identify the contestants then as well. For now, we will be concentrating on these three names. Let's start with you, Ms Samant. Why did you leave the rehearsal? Ms Rai—you are not needed now.'

I got up though I dearly would've loved to stay and hear the reason Parvati gave the Addl.CP for leaving the stage. She had told me she wanted to stretch her legs. Would she tell him the same thing? And, more importantly—*was it the truth*?

It was 10 p.m. now and I was absolutely spent. There was nothing more to be done. I decided not to wait for Parvati to finish with the Addl.CP. My legs wouldn't hold me up any longer and I shuffled tiredly to my room. Tomorrow will bring renewal, I thought. How wrong I was.

Three days to the finale ...

6

Akruti

'Do we have to go without stockings?' Roxanne, my roommate was asking, as I opened my eyes to sunshine streaming in through the window the next morning. It was a glorious sunny day, perfect, the kind you always dream about. Especially the kind you dream about when it's the day of the swimsuit round of the Miss India pageant.

For a moment I didn't remember all that had happened the night before. For a moment, drugged by sleep and sunlight, I was almost happy. Then realization hit. I checked the time—9 a.m. I had clean forgotten to set the alarm, in my weariness and anguish of the night before. I must have tumbled into bed and fallen asleep immediately in exhaustion. I hadn't even checked to see if Roxanne had come in before me or not, after being questioned by the Addl.CP.

Roxanne smiled mischievously. She had told me she was a Mumbai girl, lively and loud on occasion. Parsi undoubtedly, I could tell. Today, she was fully dressed, her six inch heels showing off those enviably smooth legs, polished to sheen with creams and concoctions. In the mirror behind her, I sleepily attempted to decipher the reflected names of each of her potions on the dressing table: Shea Butter, Cocoa, Honey-Mist, Vanilla-Bean ... Coconut Oil.

'Ms Rai,' Roxanne continued, almost malicious. 'Planning to skip the swimwear round, are we? Have you already been promised the crown this year?'

I liked Roxanne, but I also knew this side to her, to-the-point unforgiving, brutal. 'You could've woken me,' I said tartly, swinging my legs off the bed, scampering to change. The contest started in half an hour, I still had to run down for hair and make-up.

'And spoil everyone else's chances at the possibility of you giving us a walkover?' Roxanne retorted. 'We already have the decks stacked against us this year, with the magnificent Ms Rai as competitor. Why wake you?'

I threw her a mock-grimace, but I knew she had, in fact, woken me by her earlier query. She may have woken me late, but her intentions were still helpful. 'Carry your stockings,' I answered the question that had woken me up. 'You never know, you might be allowed to wear them if they're sheer.'

Hurriedly, I threw on a dress and raced to the green room downstairs near the pool area. This was where hair and make-up were being done for the swimsuit round. There was quite a crowd already inside, the humming of blow dryers and the general chatter of girls—the usual, familiar backdrop. Listening to the buzz, you could almost forget that the day before we had all been through a traumatic event. It was back to business, even though the main topic of conversation was yesterday's rehearsal.

My eyes sought the hair dresser, there was barely any time. To my relief, a wail of despair made me realize that she had found me first.

'Aa-ku!' Doreen Saldana shrieked in mock horror as she made her way towards me. 'How *late* you've come!'

'I know, I know,' I said, giving her a quick air kiss before settling myself into the chair in front of her. 'I overslept.'

'It's this terrible time,' Doreen clucked her tongue in sympathy as she deftly started loping my locks into a low bun. Then in a mock low voice: 'I hear *everyone's* a suspect ...'

I glanced at her in the mirror. Doreen was as loose-tongued as she was talented, we all knew that. She loved to gossip, but somehow things people told her never stayed secrets for long. And yet, she was the one who knew the industry's deepest mysteries. She was the one in whom everybody confided, rested their hearts darkest longings and desires. Doreen had that comfortable air that most of us crave in a confidante—simultaneously maternal and take-charge. Despite countless indiscretions, there was something about her that begged confidences.

'I guess,' I told her. 'The police are working on it.'

'They must be,' Doreen whispered sepulchral, though there was no need for it. 'Poor, lovely Lajjo. They *must* catch the culprit, Aku. *Before* the finale, *before* it becomes a huge scandal!'

I met Doreen's eyes in the mirror. I didn't reveal that I felt there was an unconventional methodology at play here—to let us all roam free today, going about our business, despite us all being suspects. But it was an unnatural situation as well.

Also, if I were to use the plainest logic as I had seen Parvati apply quite often, then even as suspects there was no place better than the hotel to confine us to. As young, single girls, one among us about to be chosen to represent our country, we were strictly chaperoned at present. Outside contact was all but forbidden, except on Sundays. Even phone calls were monitored, remember this was still a time before the easy accessibility that cell phones allowed. Maybe the Addl.CP had a reason for letting us all behave as if life could go on as usual. In this environment, he could control the proceedings.

'All the girls are a bit nervy today,' Doreen continued. 'You know how it is. But they're being matter-of-fact about going through with these rounds. What can you do?'

'Yes,' I murmured. 'What can you do?'

Doreen looked at me, her eyes narrowed in thought, her face almost fox-like in inquisitiveness. 'Who do you think did it? Y'know Aku, I have my guesses, though I hate to say so. I've been around every girl so much, doing their hair, talking closely to each one. You know people talk to me. But so much is different about this contest.'

I glanced at her, speculative and troubled. When Doreen looked like that, she often knew more than she was saying. It would come out eventually, I did not want to push her right then.

She spoke without me prompting her. 'Rules … so many rules, but they can be bent, na? In life, in contests … it's how much you can get away with.'

I wasn't sure I was following her. It was unlike Doreen to speak in riddles, and I wanted to get my hair done fast.

'I don't know,' I said. 'Karma tends to catch up.'

'Does it?' Doreen's eyes were crafty, as if she knew something unsavoury and secret. 'Does karma choose, I wonder? Between levels of wrongness? Who to correct first?'

She had me completely flummoxed. 'Whatever do you mean, Doreen?' I asked astonished. Doreen never struck me as philosophical, she was a giggly, gossipy creature, happy-go-lucky, and rather frivolous. Something had disturbed her.

'I mean who decides the level of wrongness? Is it as bad to smooth over an inconsequential rule that hurts no-one in order to fulfil a long-held ambition, as say, to do … well, whatever was done to Lajjo?' Doreen prattled. 'Take *Laddo* for instance …'

I was wrong, I decided. Doreen wasn't disturbed, this wasn't her being philosophical. It was her being chatty, obviously to share some silly gossip. I decided I wasn't interested right then, I had to concentrate on the swim-suit round.

'How's your husband?' I asked, changing the topic swiftly. This was not mere politeness. Gokul and Doreen were a team—he did make-up, she did hair. Both had formidable reputations in the industry and despite Doreen's loose tongue and oftover-familiar air, I genuinely liked them both. Gokul's taciturn efficiency was a perfect foil for Doreen's voluble vivacity. This contest was one of the few jobs where both husband-wife were not working together. Gokul had accepted an overseas commitment over the pageant this year.

'He's well,' Doreen's face lit up at the mention of her husband. 'He's sad to have missed the contest this year, but what to do? The Dubai job was double the money. He knows some of the girls here, he's worked with three of you before. But you Aku, are his favourite, he said so!'

I was only half listening. The clock hanging on the green room wall behind me had caught my attention in the mirror. It was nearing the time for the swimsuit round now. 'Tell him I said thank you for the support,' I murmured distractedly. 'Doreen, I'm going to run now, I'll do my own make-up, please tell the make-up man?'

'He's not here, he's already out, touching up the faces of the girls ready to go on stage.' Doreen said, fingers furiously at work, giving my hair the final finishing touches as she spoke.

'Fine. And thank you, Doreen!' I said, jumping up, off my chair, impulsively pecking her cheek as I dashed away, making contact for real this time, not air-kissing. 'You're just *f-a-b*!'

'Go on, hurry, and good luck Aku!' Doreen had smiled good-naturedly, her dimples transforming that plain, portly face to incredible beauty suddenly. This was my final memory of her.

Less than four hours later, Doreen was discovered in the green room, her throat slit by her own haircutting scissors. It was Parvati, in fact, who found her. Once again, as just the night before—all hell broke loose.

7

Akruti

⌒

Let me break my narrative here for a bit.

Considering the fact that Parvati was my comrade-in-arms on this quest, I think it's vital to include at-least a little bit of *her* viewpoint in my telling of the gruesome events that took place at the Miss India pageant of 1995. She was, after all, the reason I'd agreed to this ambitious plan of trying to aid the police in the hunt for Lajjo's killer. And she shared every bit of the horror and ugliness of what I was going through then. In fact—she was the one who found Doreen so viciously slain.

It is important, therefore, to present to you just how *she* felt at the time, *in her own words*. So you would know from someone other than me, just how deeply we felt ensnared—day after day, by those continually awful circumstances. And I have the best way to include her version—entries from the diary she had carefully kept at the time.

I've already mentioned how meticulous Parvati was, painstakingly jotting clues and drawings in that diary. She also scribbled her observations on the pageant as she willed, it was after all her private journal as much as a record of our progress in the investigation.

I will share what she wrote in it at certain intervals in my telling of our story. Beginning, here, with the day of Doreen's

67

death. On that particular day, Parvati's diary reflected her innermost state of mind. And I have one word for that state, I myself had been through it the night before: agitated.

From the pages of Parvati's diary

2 p.m.

Cannot come to terms with it. The sight. The terrible shock. Because it was a shock, even for me. To see her like that on the floor, her eyes wide open and staring … Her limbs too, all askew. And the blood … so much of it. All over her, all over the floor. I noticed though, almost absentmindedly in that initial jolt, how, right next to her on the floor, her haircutting scissors gleamed brightly. Not a spot on them. I need to stay focused on our search, not let the horror of seeing Doreen so brutally killed overwhelm me …

2.30 p.m.

Just can't stop thinking of it. It plays over and over in my mind. Every awful moment. Walking in to the green room, bathrobes hastily pulled over our shiny new swimsuits. The adrenalin rush of the swimsuit round still active, and Tania chattering excitedly about how she had given it her all. I, only half listening, as usual. Tend to zone out when Tania gets animated. Her constant chatter disrupts my thought process.

And then, seeing Doreen, fallen right near the dressing tables with all their full-length mirrors. Her broken body reflected in all of them, so the effect was one of many fallen Doreens. I couldn't breathe in that moment. So gut-wrenching—so horribly macabre that sight. On her lifeless face, an expression of such fear that Tania stopped mid-sentence, shocked into silence at the sight. It was I who had exclaimed, badly shaken.

3.30 p.m.

Trying to rest as we were instructed to by the chaperones, before the police start calling us for questioning again. I have to get my mind to quieten down. Need to move beyond how it felt to see her fallen so. No good will come of reliving it again and again. What I keep remembering, are Doreen's haircutting scissors. They lay next to her on the floor, gleaming unsullied. The weapon most probably used to slice her throat. So shiny because it had no doubt been wiped clean by whoever did this.

4 p.m.

Keep going over the starkness of the gore we saw today. My mind just won't let me be. Like when we first saw Doreen, Tania didn't scream. She just turned from the sight. Almost puppet-like, that movement. And then, she bent over with urgency, her mouth and body tensed, as if to throw up. She spasmed, again and again. It was all dry-retching, there was no food coming up. How could it, this was just post the swimsuit round, no one had eaten that morning to preserve the impression of flat bellies in barely-there bodices. I was the one calling out, first in terror, then for help. And I won't deny it, we were both tearful immediately —Doreen had been *such* a favourite.

Second murder in two days: that thought came unbidden, as I had bent to check Doreen's pulse. Tania began screaming then, like a raving lunatic. I didn't try and stop her. The faster help arrived, the better for Doreen, especially if, by some slim chance, there was still life left in her.

4:30 p.m.

I really need to write all this down. Just to get it out of my system. We have the time, the police haven't called us yet. Doing this might also help me see everything clearer. My brain's frozen right now with the rawness of it. Fortunate that we had both entered the green room together, Tania and I. She's forever leaving something behind somewhere and then wants to go to places escorted to retrieve it. That old sexist joke about women wanting to visit restrooms together applies entirely to her, I think. And as her roomie, mostly I'm the chosen one.

I don't mind, I rather like Tania actually. She's chilled out and laid back. Musical too, on account of her Assamese heritage, she says. She insists music is in their blood. That's one thing the *Eye India* organizers didn't take into account. Roommates would certainly figure out each other's backgrounds—it's inevitable. Anyway, Tania's funny on occasion. Not stand-offish, as many of the contestants here. Poor thing, she's a mess right now. They won't let her take a sleeping pill, we have to meet Mhatre first.

5 p.m.

The police will be calling us shortly, the chaperone phoned to tell us. I'm writing down all I recall of the sequence of events. It'll be easier that way, for me to narrate to the police when they ask. I can just hear Akruti's voice in my head: 'You're *so* methodical, Parvati. *Always* documenting.' But really—is there any other way to be?

Anyway, here goes: Tania had wanted a hairbrush, because it was windy on the ramp at the swimsuit round and she didn't want her hair a mess after. So she asked me to go with her to get it, the round had just finished. We wrapped our bathrobes hastily and walked, to the green room.

We saw Doreen as we entered. Observing her sweet face so agonized in death, the tears had come without us even noticing. Unimaginable, this situation—another murder not even twenty-four hours since Lajjo's brutal end.

At my calling out, followed by Tania's frantic and hysterical cries, help had arrived. The overall in-charge, event-coordinator Anjali Rodrigues, a large, fiery lady with avant garde electric blue streaks in her short red hair had rushed in. Known to be cool under pressure, which was important now. With her were various personnel who were present at this round.

Lubaina Pervez, our speech and diction specialist, who was to take a session with us post the swimsuit affair. We had been working with her for the past two and a half weeks, this was to be one of the final sessions, to help firm up the all-important Q&A round on the final day. To me, she always seemed another lady, like Anjali, unflappable and in control in the most manic of times.

The make-up man, Imtiaz, who was hanging around near the ramp, in case any contestant needed touch-ups, he arrived too. And Avi, who hadn't choreographed this round, but had been present for moral support.

Also accompanying them were several of the hotel staff. The swimsuit round judges, had mercifully moved to the interior of the hotel already, they weren't part of this group who came dashing up, heeding my call and the terror in Tania's desperate voice. Our chaperones were, though, looking irritated that we had left the poolside without telling them. That was before they saw Doreen.

We were escorted out immediately, Avi saw to that. Our chaperones took us to the hotel doctor to assess shock symptoms, so we didn't know what happened once the police got to the green room. So there it is, the sequence of events, as I recall them. I have to add the obvious though—One murder can be looked at as anomaly. But *two*? Two seem suspiciously veering towards the work of a serial killer. The contest is in real danger of being called off. I think all of us are conscious of it now.

8 p.m.

Finally finished yet another meeting with the sunshiny Mr Mhatre. He called for us sometime around 5.30 p.m. and we've just got done. Now we're to join the rest of the girls in the hotel hall to be instructed further by both the police and our organizers. I doubt Lubaina's speech session will happen today. Mhatre wants to speak to the other girls about Doreen, that itself will take time.

As with all of today's events, am writing down everything that transpired in our meeting in detail. Documenting it now might serve us well later, when we collate all the information we have, to help us on this search. Even if in a small way, who knows? Once more, here goes:

'Ms Parvati,' Mhatre began curtly, even as we entered the room. 'Yesterday, you helped Ms Akruti with the dead contestant, Lajjo. Today you found the dead hairdresser first. You seem to be everywhere. How is that?'

'Coincidence,' I met his eyes. 'Sheer coincidence.' Next to me Tania, quivered, I could feel her unease at Mhatre's cold assertiveness.

Also adding here what happened last night, in case I forget later: I had spoken with the Addl.CP at length post watching the rehearsal recording with Akruti. I had explained my need to 'stretch' in the thirty-second blackout when I left formation on ramp. I had 'severe cramps in my legs from the prolonged rehearsals', I had told him. I left the ramp area for a few seconds, and returned to formation very near my original place. I had made sure to appear completely confident while speaking with him.

Mhatre had tried to approach my absence from various angles, but ultimately had left it when I seemed unflappable and stuck to my story. Today he was raring to go again, I could tell.

'Tania, isn't it?' He turned to her. 'Ms Tania, you were with Ms Parvati when you saw the hairdresser?'

'Yee-es' Tania's nerves over the Addl.CP's attitude made her seem unsure, though of course we were together that morning when we found Doreen.

'You seem uncertain?' Mhatre fixated on Tania.

'Yes, I mean, no,' Tania stammered. 'We were together. Parvati was with me. We entered the green room together. We saw Doreen ... poor, poor Doreen, so much blood, all over, all over, everywhere ...'

'Everywhere?' Mhatre raised an eyebrow. 'On the floor, near the body you mean.'

'No, everywhere,' wailed Tania, sobbing openly. 'So many Doreens, so much blood!'

Mhatre looked perplexed, and I could see why. Talking like this, Tania seemed unhinged, most certainly coming apart. But I understood what she hadn't articulated from the weariness of shock.

'She means the mirrors,' I spoke up. 'Doreen fell near the dressing table mirrors. There are so many facing each other, we saw her reflected through the room. And the blood. Hence: everywhere.'

'I see,' comprehension dawned on Mhatre's dour face. 'Why were you there anyway? Where were your chaperones?'

'To get a hairbrush,' I said. 'Tania wanted one, her hair was a mess post the swimsuit round because it was windy and she'd left it loose. She's my roomie, she asked me to go with her to collect the brush from the green room. We were only to go for a minute or so. We didn't think chaperones were needed just to fetch a hairbrush.'

'And what did you see?' Mhatre asked. I described our ordeal in detail. Also, taking care to let him know about the scissors lying on the floor next to Doreen, their shiny avatar disconcertingly at odds with the blood all over the place.

'Very well,' Mhatre said, adding curtly, 'The scissors were the murder weapon in all probability. Forensics should confirm our initial report.' He was watching my face closely as he said this. Maybe he was suspicious of me because of my absence from ramp during the blackout last night. But he couldn't fault my story. Nor Tania's emphatic, if tearful assertion, that we were together when we found Doreen. He had, it seemed, already taken care to enquire about any swimsuit round recording. It was there, of course, and he would, no doubt, find me in it. In full view throughout the two hour round. There was no way I could've gotten to Doreen before the time I found her. Mhatre might be suspicious of me but he had nothing to go upon. Yet.

'Were any of you in the green room earlier?' Mhatre persisted.

'Yes, of course,' Tania stammered. 'Before the round. To get our hair done. And make-up, by Imtiaz, the make-up man.'

'And how long was the round?' Mhatre asked.

'Around two hours? Before which we were waiting for the judges to arrive,' I said.

'We will know the exact time of death from the post mortem,' Mhatre looked at us. 'Then we will meet again. To find out which of you girls were with her last. That will be all for now.'

We followed Mhatre out of the room to go join the rest in the hall outside. But my mind was restless. It's still ticking furiously now.

8.30 p.m.

Thing is—the police are doing their job. But *we* too can try to figure out who was with Doreen last. Or who could've possibly wanted her dead. And *why.*

8

Akruti

⌒

Two murders, less than twenty-four hours apart. Both at an iconic, national beauty pageant. The mind boggled, if one actually put this in perspective. I could not help but feel two things. The first: a sense of hollowness, as I had felt when Lajjo was killed the night before. Because even though Doreen wasn't close, I had liked her a lot and I missed her bright effervescence. And the second: a conviction that *somehow* this spate of horror needed resolution and I must help bring it in.

Before that, I needed to get one thing done.

I dialled the ever-familiar number hurriedly. Furtively, I might add, after all, this was *Eye India*'s rival—The *Bharat 360*, second largest newspaper in the country.

'I'd like the sports desk,' I spoke rapidly into the receiver. 'Jehaan Warrior, please. This is Akruti Rai.'

Despite the strict vigil kept on us and chaperones round the clock, I had managed to slip away from supervision to speak to someone male (*Eye India* chaperones decidedly would not be thrilled).

I had just dialled a boisterous, fun-loving someone with a wicked sense of humour and a wonderful, full-throated laugh. He happened to head the sports section at *Bharat 360*.

Dimples that lit up the room, deeper in the left cheek. An award-winning journalist and a health fanatic, the flamboyant Jehaan Warrior, *a.k.a.* my perfect, very Parsi boyfriend.

He was the person I needed to speak to right now. The one the press had not written of, as yet. Possibly because the lifestyle sections had not guessed his connect to me. But more so, I felt, out of courtesy to one of their own.

'Aku?' Jehaan's voice came on, sounding worried and tense. 'What's going on there? You alright?'

Quickly, I filled him in on the events of the past twenty-four hours. I had been too tired to speak with him before. But he already knew the drill, being generally familiar with police procedure as most mainline news journalists tend to be. He hadn't called me, waiting patiently till I could, but clearly, as part of a buzzing newsroom, he already knew of the sinister turn the contest had abruptly taken. And was weary with worry, I could tell.

'I need a favour,' I continued, once the drama and despair had been conveyed. 'I need you to do a background check on one of the contestants for me.'

'Aku?' Jehaan's voice sounded unsure. 'This is a contest where two murders just happened. You are still a participant ...'

'I don't consider her competition, you know this,' I told him. 'I need to know because she doesn't seem to be who she says she is.'

'I don't doubt you,' Jehaan's voice was patient, taut. 'But I can tell you are up to something. And if it is dangerous, if you feel she is a suspect or ought to be—I'd rather you stayed away.'

'I don't think she's a suspect, or rather, my instinct tells me she isn't,' I spoke slowly, seriously. 'But she is not who she says she is. You know how much I rely on my inner voice ...'

Jehaan didn't bother to reply, I heard him sigh.

'I need to know what she isn't telling me,' I said. '*Please*, Jehaan? It's important.'

'Be careful,' he said curtly. I knew he would do as I asked. Jehaan denied me nothing. He would route his enquiry through his various crime journalist friends and any others I didn't care to learn of. I would have my information soon enough.

'Who is the person you want me to check out?' he asked.

'Her name is Parvati,' I said. 'Parvati Samant.'

Call over, I put the receiver down with great care. I was still in the main lobby and I didn't want anyone to know I'd called Jehaan. Then I went back to the hall where all the contestants had gathered once more to await instructions. We had been sent to our rooms earlier, following the discovery of Doreen's body. Now we'd been called back down to speak to the police. They were already with Parvati and Tania. I entered the hall discreetly, noting the pall on the faces of my fellow contestants. Everyone looked shell-shocked. There was that silence that descends in a place of grieving, that deafening quietude of white noise when there is nothing to be said and yet the spirit is anxious, restless.

It was fortunate for Parvati that she had gone to the green room with Tania, or rather, both she and Tania had each other's stories to corroborate, because they had stumbled upon Doreen *together*. I hadn't had a chance to speak with Parvati yet. The morning's swimsuit round followed by the awful discovery of Doreen had us all running in circles, horror-struck and borderline hysterical in turn, before being summoned to this hall by the police.

Now, we waited for Addl.CP Mhatre, in what seemed to be a bizarre déjà vu tableau of our wait last night.

Mhatre stepped into the hall after what seemed like aeons. Following him, Parvati and Tania, both looking pale and tired.

'I will speak with each of you now,' he announced before disappearing into the room he had emerged from, the one adjoining the hall. We knew his team was in there with him as well.

Parvati found me immediately after.

I scrutinized her face. She looked pulled down, dark circles under the eyes. Clearly the Addl.CP had grilled her late into the night, the previous night, about her absence from the ramp formation in the blackout. And now, today, she was the one who found poor Doreen with Tania. No amount of make-up, however skilfully applied could hide the effects of that kind of shock.

If it was shock and not fear that was giving her dark circles. Could Parvati be hiding her real nature? *Could she indeed be a killer?*

So much seemed inexplicable about her. Hard facts battled against my instinct which stupidly was in denial. Meanwhile, if she was tired, she wasn't showing it in her behaviour.

'*Akruti*,' she hissed, gesturing for me to come away from the others to a corner. 'We have work to do.'

I went towards her, as discreetly as possible.

'The Addl.CP will soon have the time of death of Doreen,' Parvati said, matter of fact. 'We need to find out who could've been with her while we were busy on stage at the swimsuit round. Also—we need to find out *why* anyone would want her dead at all.'

I tried to recall my own hurried entry and exit of the green room just a few hours earlier. Why, I too was in the running for suspect number one again—after all, I was possibly the

last person to have got my hair done with Doreen, I had been
so late in coming down.

'Doreen knew something,' I said slowly trying to remember
our conversation. 'She was talking about ... *karma* of all
things. *Doreen!*'

'Akruti,' Parvati held my shoulders and gazed into my
eyes, her voice commanding. 'You need to recall everything
Doreen said. *Everything*. Because once again, like on ramp
when you were facing us like a camera yesterday—here too,
you may have been in a position to know something. *Without
realizing you knew it*, y'know?'

'Okay,' I said. 'I'm trying to think. She mentioned someone
in our talk on karma, I forget the name. It was a pet name
perhaps, not any of the girls, I don't think, at least we haven't
used it ... but I was only half paying attention, I wanted to
concentrate on the swimsuit round.'

Disappointment surged through me as I said this. It was
the second time I was in a position to observe things others
couldn't and I had been intent on acing the contest, not paying
attention.

'It will come to you,' Parvati said. 'Keep thinking.
Meanwhile, who do you think was with her last?'

'Me,' I said. 'Or I was one of the last. But that means
nothing. Anyone could've popped into the green room even
during the swimsuit judging. To touch up their hair and
Imtiaz was near the ramp outside but Doreen wasn't.'

'Yes,' Parvati frowned. 'We need to go over which girls
were *not* on ramp when Doreen was hurt. But for that again
... we need to know the time of death from the Addl.CP.'

'Did you know Lajjo and Nuzhat had a catfight in
the washroom yesterday?' Anuradha strolled up to us,

interrupting the conversation. Her eyes looked huge, her voice a whisper, as if sharing something illicit.

Nuzhat wasn't a popular contestant. For the past couple of weeks, she had managed to cause trouble between girls, summarily slinking away after fanning flames of discontent. I had observed this from a distance often enough, made a mental note to keep away from her.

Nuzhat's last fight had been with Tara, a girl I believe Parvati felt distinctly motherly towards. Tara had left the room in tears at the time. Parvati had quietly spoken to Nuzhat. She had looked decidedly put out after, though she said nothing.

'Lajjo claimed Nuzhat stole her eyeliner, Nuzhat said she'd only borrowed it and flung it back at her from her purse,' Anuradha confided. 'Lajjo threatened to brand her a thief, go to the contest organizers, Nuzhat told her "I'll *kill* you for this, I *will!*" Do you think she actually did?'

'How do you know about the incident?' Parvati asked Anuradha, her eyes narrow.

'A bunch of us were present—Mayuri, Tara, myself,' said Anuradha. 'And just now when the police asked us about Doreen's enemies, it suddenly came up. The shock had made us forgetful yesterday. All of us told the Addl.CP what we'd seen. The extra bit about the fight with Lajjo, though nothing about Doreen. But even if Nuzhat knifed Lajjo in a fit of anger, why would Doreen be murdered? And like this, so awfully?'

'Nuzhat was way up front, on ramp, almost next to me. And she didn't move, remember? Lajjo was walking oddly much before she even reached her,' I told Parvati quietly once Anuradha had wandered off, still dazed-looking.

'Yes, that's true,' Parvati's face was grim. 'But she's definitely a suspect on the police list if they know about the catfight.

And we need to keep an eye on her, she's a bit of a fire starter, you must know that. Look at how she targets Tara again and again. You know, a girl like her … it's possible she might not have held the knife. But Akruti, knowing her temperament— who is to say *she didn't incite someone else into doing that*? If she did, she's also culpable. Possibly—*a mastermind*.'

'No connect to Doreen though,' I said, partially horrified at the word picture Parvati had just painted. Such evil chilled me to the bone and I was already nervy, as were we all.

'Yes, that's true,' Parvati' acquiesced. 'No connect to Doreen. We really need to know Doreen's time of death to decide how to proceed next. But looks like the police *do* have a concrete possible suspect for Lajjo's murder …'

9

Akruti

Doreen was murdered between 10 and 11 a.m. that morning, the closest the post mortem (conducted very fast as such cases go) could decide, as to time of death. The swimsuit round was to begin at 9.30 a.m., and didn't begin before 10.15 a.m., when all the judges had arrived. It went on for almost two hours. Around 12.30 p.m. or so, Parvati and Tania had approached the green room together, seeking a hairbrush, and instead endured yet another awful brush with death, for the second time in 24 hours.

So, between 10 a.m. and 10.15 a.m. when all the girls were required to be onstage—anyone could've had the opportunity to slip into the green room and stab Doreen. In all probability, she had been stabbed then, and stabbed with her haircutting scissors, the police were quite certain (Forensics would confirm later). This was Addl.CP Mhatre's understanding of the murder and we were privy to it so as to recount our individual actions in that timeframe.

Eye India could not hush up any of this. The first murder had been shocking enough, now there were two. There were not as many news channels in 1995 then as there are today, else there would've been mayhem on the airwaves.

But *Bharat 360* had made sure Lajjo's death the night before was front page news that following day, even as *Eye India* publications sought to downplay the attention. The next day's papers would be a riot, there could be no more possibility of downplaying anything.

There was a series of meetings at the highest levels, between the *Eye India* bosses and the police. *Eye India* did not want to cancel or postpone the contest. Their sponsors were eager to continue. The pressure on the police to catch the killer, or come up with a possible suspect was tremendous. And it trickled down to the Addl.CP who looked grimmer with each passing hour.

There was more to fuel his woes. Our families had been contacted, and many were up in arms, wanting to take their daughters out of the contest. My own parents, always trusting of my decisions uptil now, were beside themselves with worry. As was Jehaan.

'Aku, do you *have* to continue with this?' my worried mother asked, even as my father, normally cool with my most hair-raising exploits, practically shouted into the receiver to stop with this foolhardiness and come home.

It took all my patience to convince them that I *needed* to stay on. I had not let on that I, as all the others were also suspects, now in *both* murders, so would possibly not have been allowed to leave the premises anyways, without police permission.

I doubt many of the girls had underlined this in their conversation with their families. It was a strange time indeed—our fairy-tale dreams were becoming increasingly difficult to sustain in the face of the morbid reality we were now part of. And there was pressure on many levels—parental as well as police, not to mention the actual pressure of wanting to place well at the contest.

As of now though, no one was pulling out. Despite worried entreaties from those back home, all twenty girls stayed put. We all wanted our shot at the crown if the contest was to continue. And no doubt the police wanted us all at one place so they could finish their job.

All of us, that is, with the exception of Avi. He had been given special permission to leave the premises later that day and all of the following as well, to confer with *Eye India's* national head honchos who had flown in from the capital to join the regional CEO.

It was he and not the overall event coordinator Anjali Rodrigues who had to meet the bosses, because he was the one present, directing the finale rehearsal when Lajjo was stabbed. He also had some explaining to do, I guessed, as to why he had dialled the Mumbai police himself, leaving his aide to inform his paymasters, right after Lajjo's murder. The police no doubt trusted his credentials enough for him to leave and return, he had been the one to call them first, after all. Or perhaps strings had been pulled so he might leave for a while, to brief the bosses. Whichever it was, Avi was gone for the next two days, at least.

'So, Akruti,' Parvati caught hold of me again. 'Any leads?'

'I left the green room at 9.20 a.m., maybe,' I told Parvati. 'There were still several girls in the room then, and some others were flitting in and out. This looks like an impossible task to pinpoint ...'

'Nothing is impossible,' Parvati said, her pen and diary already posed for notation. 'Name the girls you saw at 9.20 a.m. ...'

'Pia, Sanjna, Inayat ... Aishwarya,' I tried to recall the background during my chat with Doreen that morning. 'They were almost done. I think Inayat was left to go after me, she was waiting impatiently, I noticed her expression. I think some went to find Imtiaz, so he could retouch their make-up. Also, Roxanne came in once and left again immediately. I still hadn't finished with Doreen.'

'We need to speak with Inayat,' Parvati's voice was decisive. 'She would've been one of the last to see Doreen alive.'

Inayat was twenty years old, harbouring dreams of wanting to get into interior decoration someday. She had a boyfriend who was from a Bollywood family and she wouldn't stop gushing about him. Other than her twin obsessions—interior design and her Bollywood boyfriend—she didn't seem particularly ambitious.

I suspected her presence in this pageant was more her boyfriend pushing to have an arm-candy beauty queen, than any real desire on Inayat's part. At present, she was leaning into a couch settee, awaiting her turn with the Addl.CP.

'There she is,' I pointed out. 'Let's do this already.'

If we thought quizzing Inayat would be a delicate affair, we were pleasantly mistaken. She started talking as soon as we approached her.

'Horrible, *no*?' she whispered as we walked up to the couch, making ourselves comfortable on either side of her. 'I just can't believe it. Doreen was *such* a sweetheart. Who would want to do this to her?'

'Who indeed?' Parvati echoed. 'Did she seem worried or scared when she did your hair, Inayat?'

'No, not at all!' Inayat said. 'She was her usual pleasant self. She was joking with me about Kush, that's Kushwant my B.F., you know? He's going to be in a movie soon, and she was talking about how she's glad he got his break so fast. People struggle for years to get a break in movies. Even though Kush's parents are filmdom royalty, he's determined to prove himself on his own. I'm soooo proud of him …'

'Yes, of course,' Parvati showed interest and Inayat continued, eager to recount her boyfriend's victories. 'Doreen said she was happy because she's seen how people struggle to get somewhere, sometimes for years. Why, even in this pageant she said there might have been a struggle if rules hadn't been bent.'

'What do you mean?' I couldn't keep the sharpness out of my voice. 'What rules were bent? *For whom?*'

'There are some really silly rules in the pageant, Akruti,' Inayat turned her big dark eyes to me, most gratified to have found an audience. With a pang, I realized that I hadn't really bothered to converse much with other contestants earlier. At least, not in this intimate and gossipy way.

'Doreen said she knew someone at the contest had gotten in by bending the rules,' Inayat continued. 'She said it hadn't hurt anyone, so why not?'

Parvati's eyes met mine over Inayat's head. I remembered suddenly that Doreen had been saying something about bending rules when we were talking of karma too.

'In fact, had these rules not been bent, this contestant would never have been allowed to participate,' Inayat said. 'And it was her dearest dream to be in this contest, imagine. Just like Kush's, to become an actor. That's why Doreen said she was glad Kush got his chance so easily. Some people can't, na? Even if they have the potential, there is no luck. Then they have to go around rules, break rules …'

'Who was she talking of, Inayat, can you remember?' Parvati asked softly.

'She said the name and the music testing for the swimsuit round came on, over the mic outside. There was a sudden crash of sound, so I didn't hear her properly,' Inayat said easily, as yet unaware as to what a big almost-revelation she was making right then.

'Do you know what rule was being bent?' Parvati asked, her voice so silky I was mesmerized. I realized later that this was Parvati's special voice, the one she seemed to use when on the scent of something potentially big.

'Y'know the rule which says relatives of employees of *Eye India* or mentors of the contest cannot participate in the pageant? It is such a silly rule,' said Inayat. 'Do you mean to tell me if my uncle is working at *Eye India*, I shouldn't try for a shot at the crown? What nonsense! It's such a silly rule, na? But it's taken so seriously by the organizers.'

'*So there is someone in the contest who ought not to be here?*' Parvati's expression was grim.

'Yes if you put it that way,' Inayat's expression seemed slightly alarmed now. 'The organisers want to seem impartial I think. But it's a silly rule, anyway.'

'Was there anything else you discussed?' Parvati asked, still smooth-voiced.

'No, there wasn't any time. There were two or three others waiting for a quick touch up—Pia, Aishwarya. Also, Sanjna was hanging around, waiting for Pia to finish. Doreen finished my hair quickly, I got up and ran to change. I didn't know it would be our last conversation ...' Inayat, ready to chat so far, now looked stricken at the memory. There was a sudden silence.

Parvati grabbed the opportunity to pull me off the couch. 'We have willy-nilly stumbled onto something important,' she said. 'A rule was bent—one the organisers take seriously. Poor loose-tongued Doreen knew who had bent that rule and was chatting about it freely to anybody who would listen. Obviously, the contestant in question wanted it to be kept secret, if she was found out, she would be disqualified. And from what Inayat says, being here was a very special dream for this person. So, *who was that person*? And could she be disturbed enough about Doreen's gossip to *kill* her? Did she feel she had that much to lose, really?'

'That's really scary, Parvati,' I told her, sombre and troubled. 'We need to tell the police this.'

'I just remembered!' Inayat broke into our whispering, as she walked up. 'Someone else was calling for Doreen too, I heard the voice as I got up from my seat. It came from behind the green room curtain, one of the cubicles there. So there was Pia, Aishwarya, Sanjna and someone else. I couldn't see the fourth girl, but Doreen even answered her. She said, "There are others before you. So you'll have to wait, *Laddo*."'

'OMG,' I could barely hold my interjection till Inayat turned away. 'That's the name, Parvati. The one Doreen mentioned when she spoke of karma. A pet name—*Laddo*.'

'Are you sure?' Parvati looked at me searchingly, keen eyes boring into mine.

'Yes, yes,' I said, recalling my conversation with Doreen. 'Absolutely. She said "*Laddo*". And she said it in the context of levels of karma ... she asked who decided levels of karmic retribution. How wrong was it to gloss over a rule if it hurt no one and would fulfil a long-held ambition ... and she mentioned this name, she was going to go further in telling me the story, but I was not interested ...'

'You realise that this *Laddo* might have been listening to Doreen all the while, don't you?' Parvati said. 'As she spoke to Inayat so casually about something so vital to her. And Doreen spoke to you too, only you didn't bother to go further ... *which might actually have saved your life*.'

The import of her words dawned on me. If what Parvati was saying was true, *Laddo*, whoever she was, might indeed be a killer. Sitting there, waiting her turn behind one of the cubicle curtains in the green room, and overhearing Doreen spill an important secret that would spoil her chances at the contest. At her *dearest dream*, at the event she had wanted to be part of so much, that she had *already risked breaking rules* to enter. Which meant Inayat could still be in danger herself … suppose she recognized the voice or remembered something else of significance?

We need to talk to the Addl.CP right now,' Parvati said grimly, having read my face. 'But also to Sanjna, Aishwarya and Pia … Who knows what they saw or heard. Do you know who this person might be, with the pet name of *Laddo* in this contest, by the way?'

'Not a clue,' I said. 'But I barely speak to the others. We should try and ask around after we speak to the police.'

We walked into the room where the Addl.CP had just finished with another contestant. He didn't seem surprised to see us at all. Or it was just his nature, dour and unruffled, come what may.

'I see,' he said, once Parvati finished her story, narrated briefly and to the point. 'This information is timely. We will speak to all these contestants. And provide protection to the girls you named, if necessary.'

He didn't ask us how we stumbled on this information, nor did he seek to prevent us from uncovering more. I wondered how much pressure he was under, that it didn't occur to him to stop two foolhardy young girls, clearly out of their depth, from stepping into a murder investigation way over their heads. I didn't know at that time what he knew about Parvati then. I would find out soon enough when Jehaan called me later. But I had that night to get through first.

Before which, we actually managed to speak with all three girls—Pia, Aishwarya and Sanjna.

As we left Addl.CP Mhatre in his corner room, we bumped into the trio—or rather Pia and Sanjna walking past, Aishwarya was seated on a chair quite close by.

'Hey girls, how's it going?' Parvati called out to them. They stopped and greeted her immediately. It occurred to me that competitive and intent on winning as I was, I may not have really bothered to speak to the rest of the contestants during the first few weeks of our time together. But Parvati, down-to-earth and unassuming, had a lot of goodwill going for her.

'We might have been the last to see her,' Pia confided mournfully, straight to the heart of what each of us was feeling. She was from an army background, an intelligent, articulate girl, well-travelled and worldly. No wonder she and Sanjna, a techie with an American accent (Sanjna had schooled abroad from a young age) got along well.

'Yes, we had our hair touched-up last, I think,' Sanjna chimed in. 'Us and Ashu.' She pointed to Aishwarya sitting nearby, who got up and walked over to us slowly. Aishwarya was an enigma, a girl, who like me, kept to herself. But solace in numbers was better now, rather than flying solo, we needed each other for security and comfort in this uncertain time.

I remembered suddenly how Sanjna hadn't been anywhere near her place in the formation on ramp last night either. But Parvati pre-empted me.

'Sanjna, how come you weren't in your place on ramp last night?' Parvati's direct query was perhaps the best way to address this. 'I came back to find my place had shifted. *You* had taken it!'

Sanjna looked uncomfortable. For a moment I doubted her intensely, then she blurted, 'I wanted to be as far away as *possible* from Nuzhat. She was bothering me. I saw your place empty during that blackout, I took the chance, I *really* needed to, Parvati, I'm *so* sorry …'

Nuzhat again. All of us understood immediately. In every walk of life, there are always the 'mean girls'. Sometimes, just the one. That trouble maker, the person who taunts and teases and bullies those weaker, unanimously disliked, barely tolerated.

Nuzhat was most certainly emerging as the bad apple in this lot of girls. Let me describe her in detail so you get a picture: an unpleasant person, rake-thin and wizened-looking, like a dried prune. No doubt some circles thought her lovely, her body all sharp angles, her eyebrows in thin lines, pout perfected with lip pencil to appear as sourly exacting as herself. She was quick to seek out weakness and play on it, sharp-tongued, simpering-malicious, in fact, often downright nasty.

All of us handled her in our own ways. She hadn't dared to trouble me to my face, but I had heard enough during this contest to recognise all the jealous rumour-mongering and its source. The softer girls suffered. Sanjna, one of the youngest in this contest, among them.

Yesterday's gruelling rehearsal had frayed nerves, Sanjna might have really had enough, didn't want to endure Nuzhat a second longer, even if it meant inciting Avi's temper. So, seeing a chance, she seized it and shifted her place further away just this once. An incongruous act during a regular rehearsal, but because of Lajjo's stabbing, rendered full of meaning.

'Nuzhat was two girls away, always trying to get the girls behind and in front of me to trip me up, whispering things about my Western accent as well. I had had enough,' Sanjna was saying. 'Really, yesterday was so long and tiring, I thought it's just one time, some relief …'

Parvati hugged her spontaneously. I was a tad taken aback by Parvati's artless show of affection, her impulsive kindness towards Sanjna. Such camaraderie with others never came easy to me and my supermodel status was the barrier I often hid behind. 'How was I to know what would happen to Lajjo?' Sanjna added.

'Or to Doreen,' Pia said. 'How could we ever *imagine* being involved in such a mess?'

'Who was last to get their hair done?' Parvati asked Pia, deceptively casual, her tone silky as before.

'Ashu,' Pia said. 'We were getting it done superfast, for once Doreen wasn't talking much, it was so close to the round and only three of us left to touch-up.'

'Yes, touch-ups were super quick,' Sanjna added.

'So you guys didn't chat?' I asked, entering the conversation for the first time.

'Yes, about our hair, we did. Pia's stubborn locks, my wispy fringe,' Sanjna replied, turning to me curiously. I think it suddenly occurred to them that sensible Parvati and showy me made for an unlikely duo.

'There was someone whose hair Doreen did, after mine,' Aishwarya spoke up quietly, addressing Parvati. 'She did mine very quickly. There was a girl sitting behind the green room curtain. Doreen told her told her to wait till we finished.'

'Who was she?' Parvati asked Aishwarya, her voice soft and low. I got the sense these two would be able to understand each other without words, the way discreet, introspective people all over the world sometimes do.

'I don't know, she was behind the curtain,' Aishwarya said. 'Doreen addressed her as *Laddo*. We were all so preoccupied with our looks and hair and getting costumes on. We weren't paying attention.'

'We don't know who that could be,' Pia said, Sanjna nodding her ignorance.

Just then Aishwarya was called in to meet the Addl.CP and Pia and Sanjna too walked away from us. Our conversation might have been casual on the surface. But we had another vital confirmation—apart from Inayat's narration, we were now told by more witnesses that there had been a fourth girl waiting to get her hair done. *Who might have had reason to wish Doreen dead.* We needed to find out who in the contest was called *Laddo*.

Parvati was busy scribbling all we had found out so far in her diary. 'Let's formulate a plan to find out who *Laddo* is,' Parvati said. 'Now, if possible.'

'Sure,' I said. 'We had to attend that speech class by Lubaina Pervez post this meet with the Addl.CP, right? But when are they scheduling it for, now that this is taking so long?'

'It's been pushed to tomorrow,' Parvati said. 'They announced it earlier. Maybe we can ask the girls then. We can divide it among ourselves. We'll do that.'

We were suddenly aware that someone was behind us.

'Let me pass, girls,' Nuzhat said, her expression unpleasant as she moved between us.

'You think she heard us?' I asked Parvati.

'Doesn't matter if she did,' Parvati retorted. 'She wasn't in the green room, she was on stage—first performer for the swimsuit round, we catwalked for it in random order, remember? Whatever might have happened with Lajjo, Doreen couldn't have been Nuzhat's doing. She was too busy trying to look her best, she was first up after all. And as she was nowhere near the green room, she couldn't be the *Laddo* we need to find.'

'Would be too easy, otherwise, wouldn't it?' I said lightly, though my thoughts were filled with foreboding. Were the two murders linked? They didn't seem to be. But what if there really *was* a serial killer on the loose? How on earth could we join the dots and find this person?

We parted, and since we'd met the Addl.CP already, were allowed to go to our rooms. It was nearing 10 p.m. now, and it had been a long day. I ordered room service, realised my roomie Roxanne hadn't come in yet, and retired to bed. The talent round of the pageant was on for the next day. Despite all that had happened, the contest was never too far from my thoughts.

I must have drifted off to sleep, because suddenly, I was dreaming. A faceless, formless being, draped in a veil from head to toe was hovering over me. In one hand it clutched haircutting scissors, shiny and clean. I gazed at it, wordless, terrified. As it moved towards me, its reflection emerged, multiple images, so the place seemed a mirrored room. So many images of that one ghoul, they all appeared to be surrounding me. Oddly, as it came closer, the veil slipped slightly, revealed a gown, red and sweat-stained. Its face remained veiled, like a bride. The scissors in its hand turned into a knife, dripping scarlet. 'You asked for *Laddo*?' it whispered, sepulchral, close to my face and holding a gilded crown in its other hand. Cold, clammy fingers reached for me, its veil flying off revealing …? At this point I awoke, screaming. It was morning already and the phone in the room was ringing off the hook.

Two days to the finale ...

10
Akruti

⌒

'Aku?' Jehaan's dear, soothing voice filtered through, over the receiver as I picked up the phone, half-panicked still from that awful nightmare. 'Did I wake you? It's almost 9 a.m.'

For once, phone calls were being allowed, worried families had insisted that *Eye India* lift the embargo on calls at least, so as to keep a check on the girls' safety. We had been briefed by the Addl.CP the previous day, about speaking only to family members and not entertaining the press. This also had a legal angle, as we were all still suspects.

'I'm glad you did,' I said, glancing over at Roxanne, who had turned away from me and pulled the pillow over her head once I silenced the phone's shrill ring. Clearly, she had had a bad night as well, and was in no hurry to get up.

'I needed to wake up,' I told Jehaan. 'We have a session with the speech and diction mentor, Lubaina Pervez at noon today. And the talent round of the contest happens this evening, at 6 p.m.'

'It's unbelievable they're still continuing with the show!' Jehaan sounded incredulous. 'After two murders and the possibility of a serial killer at large on the premises.'

'The organizers feel that the show must go on,' I said. 'In case this turns out to be some sort of attempt by competitors to sabotage the contest name itself. They need to stand strong they feel …'

'Come off it, Aku,' Jehaan's voice was impatient. 'You know you don't believe that propaganda. This is just about money— junking the contest at this stage would mean loss of several crores to those that matter.'

Jehaan was right, I wasn't interested, nor did I really believe *Eye India*'s propaganda. After all, Jehaan himself was from a rival newsroom and I really didn't think *Bharat 360* would go to such manic lengths to sabotage a rival company's property, as to take lives of two young women in the attempt.

But that the contest was still on worked for me. I could still help in any way possible to find out the identity of the person who had murdered Lajjo and Doreen so gruesomely. And I still had a shot at the crown for 1995.

'Whatever their reasons, I'm glad the contest is still on,' I told Jehaan. 'And I'm glad you and my parents are pretending to be understanding in letting me stay on and compete despite all that has happened.'

'You wouldn't listen, even if we wanted you to pull out,' Jehaan said dryly. 'So let's not go there. But it's dangerous, Aku. I don't think you realise how much. For you, especially. Because you are the most high-profile contestant this year. And you caught Lajjo as she fell. Seen today's headlines yet?'

'No,' I said warily, suddenly worried. 'Are they very damaging?'

'There's certainly a lot of publicity, only natural for a crime of this proportion.' Jehaan was being realistic, I knew the news couldn't be good. But there were more important things to worry about.

'I'm fine, if that's why you called,' I told him.

'Glad to hear that. Also, you wanted to know about a contestant,' Jehaan cut right to the chase. 'Parvati Samant?'

I moved closer to the receiver, hushed my voice. It would not do to have Roxanne listen in on this conversation. She seemed to have gone back to sleep though.

'An interesting person, this Parvati,' Jehaan was saying. I held my breath. Would my instinct be wrong this time? *Would Jehaan tell me she had a criminal record or a sordid past?*

'Her father is chief of RAW.'

'WHAT?!' I gasped at Jehaan's words. RAW, India's formidable Research and Analysis Wing, the external intelligence outfit established with a view to strengthen our nation against foreign terror, espionage and the like. As far as I knew, RAW was accountable singularly and only to the office of the Prime Minister of India. Shadowy, secretive, extremely powerful ... a lot like Parvati, it seemed.

'She's not your average beauty contestant for sure, Aku,' Jehaan went on. 'Though with that kind of lineage, I doubt very much that she's a murderer.'

Now it all made sense. Parvati's low key demeanour, her exacting notes, her diary, her comfort in speaking with the police, despite her youth. She had possibly grown up watching her father deal with such stuff. And the Addl.CP's seeming nonchalance at her repeated intervention into an on-going investigation. I wondered exactly how much he knew about Parvati.

'Aku, it could be that she had ambitions of becoming a beauty queen,' Jehaan continued. 'But it also seems a hell of a coincidence that she was contesting at the same pageant where two murders just happened to take place, one after another ... It is *too* much of a coincidence, if you ask me. And that makes everything even more dangerous ...'

'You mean she was here on work related to RAW? That's absurd. She's 19,' I said, but even to my ears, I was sounding unconvinced.

It made sense that Parvati would be here helping her father out for some reason. She had never seemed the glamorous type to me, not from the very start of this pageant. With the right make-up, she was actually rather gorgeous in a healthy, basic kind of way. But if she was here to help her dad in some manner—that would mean the contest was compromised on several levels, possibly to do with national security?

'It's scary to think like that,' I confided to Jehaan. What connection could RAW have to a beauty contest, of all things?'

'I'm still figuring that one out,' Jehaan admitted. 'It's actually beyond the realms of comprehension, the two seem so unrelated! And yet, the only daughter of the chief of RAW, a serious and studious young lady I'm told, has suddenly decided to participate in a beauty pageant. This, in the year closely following the ones which had massive riots and blasts in the city.'

'Put like that, it is even scarier,' I told Jehaan sombrely. His journalist's mind could analyse every occurrence to its bare bones and I was at time discomfited by it.

'Be careful, Aku,' Jehaan warned, his tone at once concerned and frustrated. He knew I would never let go now.

'You think she had me screened?' I asked him. 'She requested we work together, you know.'

'It could all be just coincidence,' Jehaan demurred. 'She is, after all, as you said, only nineteen. I doubt the RAW head would want his daughter involved in anything dangerous.'

'Thanks for this, Jehaan,' I whispered fervently. 'At least I know now my instinct is seldom wrong. She isn't a killer, she's a hunter … but *who* is she hunting?'

Whilst on the subject of hunting, I told him about my dream that night, how I woke up screaming in fear.

'Seems to me your dream is telling you something,' Jehaan said light-heartedly, after sympathizing with my trauma. I loved that about him, as I loved everything else—his ability to tell my various moods apart, his dimples, deeper in one cheek … his down-to-earth steadiness in my sometimes-superficial world of glitz.

'Your dream murderer seemed ghostly, Aku,' Jehaan laughed, 'But it was also … *a contestant,* wasn't it? *Wearing a crown, or holding one*? Is that what your subconscious is saying to you?'

'I didn't think of that,' I said to him, deeply troubled. It was true, we were all suspects.

'Are you going to chat all day?' Roxanne suddenly screeched, throwing at me the pillow she had been cradling, and breaking my cosy comfort zone with Jehaan. 'It's nearly 10 a.m. We need to get dressed for the speech session.'

I rang off hastily, assuring Jehaan that I would be careful and promising to call when I could.

As I got up to get dressed for the afternoon session with Lubaina Pervez, I found myself contemplative. Parvati and Jehaan, both of them were awakening a latent gift in me. My power of observation and retention had always been strong.

But to combine analysis and instinct—I was learning this here and now. And new as it was, It was a heady feeling. Perhaps it wasn't just Parvati on the hunt any longer.

11

Akruti

'Hurry up, we don't want to be late,' Roxanne urged as I headed to the shower, still contemplative about my dream. We were expected to help our roommates, arrive at sessions with them if possible. Roxanne had got ready before me at supersonic speed. She was nervous about the Q & A round on finale night and didn't want to miss Lubaina Pervez's session under any circumstance.

I knew Lubaina wouldn't begin until all the girls were in the room. This was her last session with us. The finale was in two days, and if you were the nervous sort and thought of it as the day after tomorrow, you got butterflies in your stomach.

I had enjoyed Lubaina's earlier sessions, in the entire two and a half weeks preceding this one. She was an elegant lady, a long-time theatre personality. The Q&A round, of course, was considered the most important in the pageant.

In fact, this year's contest was her return to pageantry. She used to be a consistent mentor at the Miss India contest for years and years, but one year ago she had gone through personal tragedy and had withdrawn from mentorship.

Rumour had it that Lubaina had lost her twenty-year-old daughter in a botched surgery, but no one knew the details. Anyway, a year later, i.e. this year, she was back, and as cool and collected as before, her skin smooth and her voice well-modulated. She didn't seem as if she had suffered tremendous loss at all. Of course, she never smiled, but a lot of people never smiled. In our own group Nuzhat, only ever smiled in malice.

Under Roxanne's watchful gaze, I was ready soon enough. I wore a sunshiny-yellow dress, and slathered on the sun block, in case we had the session outdoors. As we grabbed our keys to leave the room, I realized the morning's papers had been slipped through the door. And with a start, I remembered what Jehaan had mentioned about the news.

'*Murders Most Foul: Is there a serial killer on the loose?*' asked one headline, graphics alongside in lurid red. The other simply screamed '*Game of Terror: Hairdresser killed at Miss India,* and below that, '*Day after top model Akruti Rai caught first victim Lajwati Khan as she collapsed, hairdresser stabbed to death'.*

Sickened, I left the papers on the floor where they were. Of course, they would make sure my name was there—I was the contest's most visible face, an instant draw for audiences. But I didn't want to upset myself by reading anything more just then. I would go through them later, see if the journalists covering this story had any information we hadn't yet got.

As we all congregated in the hall, there was a sense of barely-suppressed panic. The hotel's phones were ringing off the hook—it could just be guests, but we believed the calls were from our families and dear ones, who had just woken up to the day's headlines. And perhaps the press, asking repeatedly for more information. No one was in the mood for small talk, hastily our chaperones escorted us to a smaller room where we would be addressed by Lubaina.

We were all outfitted for a sunny day, in dresses and minimal make-up. Lubaina walked in, her own appearance belying her age, which was close to fifty-five I think. She too was in a dress, formal black, and high pumps. With pearls around her throat, the complete look matched her salt and pepper French bun.

She seemed classy and confident, exactly how a mentor ought to look. Earlier on in the contest, I had had a distinct sensation of having seen her somewhere, but I couldn't place quite where. As her face grew more familiar with daily sessions, I allowed that feeling to subside. Maybe she had been a model in her youth and I had noticed her, growing up. Whatever it was, I rather liked her cool hauteur and the practised professionalism with which she encouraged us.

'I know it's been a shock,' she addressed us, after doing a quick head count to check that we were all in the room. 'But the show must go on.' Clearly, the pageant's propaganda had found its mark in her.

'So let's address the Q & A round now. Random questions will be asked to you by judges, and you must all come across as poised, intelligent and confident.'

'There will be only five of us for that,' Vanessa, or Nessie as she was called here, spoke up. 'The five among us who make it to the final round.'

We all knew when Nessie spoke, courtesy her distinct, posh British accent from schooling in a private institution. A curvaceous girl, with honey-smooth, unblemished skin, she had also won the Miss India Dream Smile pre-contest held some months ago. To me, though, she was now the girl who, along with Smriti, had taken a restroom break at a crucial juncture and shifted the entire formation on ramp the day Lajjo died.

'Yes, indeed,' Lubaina turned to her, courteous if unsmiling. 'It is my intention that, in this session, each of you think of yourselves as part of that final five.'

'When the judges ask us the questions, do we address them by their names?' Vandana, outspoken and devil-may-care, addressed Lubaina now. From what she let on, Vandana's father was a heavyweight politico, but she wanted the crown on her own terms and told us she had entered the contest without telling her parents.

Plain ambition marked her every move, but how could we hold that against her? We were all here to win. Could she be the elusive *Laddo*? I wondered. Did she know anyone here, had she bent any rules to be here, besides not telling her parents?

'That is up to you,' Lubaina said. 'But basic courtesy, such as a 'Good Evening' to the judge asking you a question, always helps set the mood. You might be nervous up there, so if you decide to just hear the judge's question and answer without preamble—that's okay too.'

I caught Parvati's eye. She was bored, I could tell. I knew she wanted to pinpoint *Laddo*'s identity. But we needed to sit through this session first.

'What if you don't know an answer or suddenly get cold feet?' Mayuri, a doe-eyed, sing-song voiced ingénue, asked hesitantly. She was a waif-like beauty, her claim to fame among us being a high society boyfriend from Pune's old money-horsing circles.

'When in doubt, *don't* shout it out!' Lubaina parroted her favourite homily. 'Stay centred, take a moment. Who will demonstrate this for me? Shilpi, sorry, Nina?'

We all giggled. Lubaina was forever calling Nina by this name, we figured it was because she resembled a contestant from one of Lubaina's earlier pageants.

'Yes,' Nina stood up. A tanned, muscular girl, she was the one who had fainted when Lajjo was stabbed. I had wondered how on earth she could be a student of medicine as she claimed she was, if she swooned at the first sight of blood. She seemed timid, which belied her stocky build. She was the one who had emphasized the fact that we were all suspects.

Her roommate, Nisha, was an effervescent, high-spirited girl. She was the exact opposite of Nina, and she always complained that she was tormented by Nina's loud music from Hindi movies whenever they were together in the room. Nina was in this contest for one reason only—to win so she could meet her idol, the Bollywood superstar SRK, a. k. a. Saurav Roop Kamal. Posters of SRK hung all over her half of their shared room.

'Nisha and Nina are at it again,' the girls used to laugh, overhearing heated voices from their room on that floor. In fact, floor lore had it, Nina had actually met SRK in her small town somewhere in the interiors of north India when he was shooting for a film. The *Eye India* bosses might want to keep regions, religion and background out of the picture publically, but in a small group of girls thrown together, certain things were bound to be brought up.

Anyway, to get to the heart of the matter, so overcome was Nina by SRK that she had vowed to come to Mumbai and meet him here. Unbelievable, that a small-town girl had actually gotten into the final twenty of the contest now, inching towards her starry dream. Even if Nisha made her disdain of her roommate clear, I was actually quite taken by the story of Nina's grit thus far.

Lubaina asked her a mock question and Nina replied with pauses, imitating someone nervous, but holding forth despite it.

'Try and appear confident, even if you aren't,' Lubaina's strong, deep voice permeated every corner of that room as she instructed us. She wanted us to speak just like she did.

As she spoke and took the session further, my mind wandered. Absent-minded, I looked outside the huge bay window at the lawn. Normally there would be no one there, hotel guests weren't allowed around us now, this area was curtailed off. Only the chaperones, and I knew them all, or members from the organizing or sound and lights team, and I knew them too.

But today there was a stranger on the lawn. Of average height, salt-and-pepper hair, cut close. Nondescript clothes, a tee and khakis, over sneakers—a person who wanted to blend in, not stand out. I being the prima donna of making entries, understood the importance of an outfit in making someone stand out.

Addl.CP Mhatre? No, it was definitely not him. A cap pulled low over the eyes, disguising his face. A policeman in plainclothes? Possible, but why alone? Mhatre's team hung around in twos and threes, I had noticed this.

The stranger looked around and seemed to be making mental notes. Then, as often happens when you are watching someone, his gaze was drawn through the window, straight at me. The glass was not one way, I was sure he could see me. And he had noticed me, watching him. At this point, almost serendipitously, the session broke for a restroom break. I edged cautiously towards the window, hoping to get closer to catching a better glimpse of him.

'Akruti, we have work to do,' Parvati suddenly appeared in the way, blocking my access to the window, impatient and restless.

Distracted, my gaze lifted, and when I looked again, the stranger was gone. Who was he? Could he be the person this mysterious *Laddo* was related to?

'There was someone outside,' I told Parvati. 'Someone who looked rather suspicious, I've never seen him before.'

Parvati's expression reflected something inscrutable, a brief, fleeting hesitation, I thought, but I may have imagined it. She appeared brisk and efficient the next second, having looked through the window.

'There's no one there,' she said. 'Might have been a journalist, looking for a scoop, y'know how they manage to get through the tightest security. Come, Akruti, let's concentrate on finding *Laddo*.'

But just then Samantha rushed up, excited. 'They're announcing the winner of the swimsuit round. Miss India Perfect 10! Come quick!'

This was rather unorthodox, contest winners were announced immediately after the contest, but in this case Doreen's unexpected and gruesome murder had changed the format yesterday. It had happened before they could announce the winner, so the results were to be unveiled today.

Lubaina Pervez had come back to the room. 'Girls, we are more or less done. Let your chaperones know, should you need to meet me again. They have yesterday's contest winners. Should we all go to the hall, please?'

Parvati raised her eyebrows in impatience. She wanted to quiz the girls about *Laddo*, but there appeared to be too much happening.

'In the hall,' I mouthed, to pacify her. 'We'll talk to the rest then ...' But in the meanwhile, I already had butterflies in my stomach. The swimsuit round was very important in that it meant additional points towards the main tally on the final day, the maximum amount of points for a pre-contest, in fact. And despite everything that had happened thus far ... *I* still wanted to win.

12

From the pages of Parvati's diary

12:30 p.m.

We've been asked to relocate to the hall in five minutes, Lubaina's session is over, thank God. Sitting through it was difficult. The Miss India Perfect 10, i.e. the swimsuit round winner is to be announced in the hall.

Akruti is looking nervous, but I'm almost sure she'll clinch this one. All I want to do is get to who *Laddo* is. Wonder if the police know by now, especially after we briefed the Addl. CP yesterday?

1 p.m.

Akruti has swept the Miss India Perfect 10 title. In all this mayhem, the first serious title, because winning this one means 40 extra points towards the final tally. Everyone is looking like they knew the result, but I think Akruti herself wasn't as sure. She looks relieved now, air kissing and waving, walking around with that sash and flowers. Good, she seems more relaxed, because I need help in sorting out the *Laddo* conundrum. The key lies there, I'm certain.

1:30 p.m.

My list of suspects for Lajjo's stabbing:

All the girls who were off-stage in that thirty-second blackout. At present: zero.

I followed Smriti and Vanessa when I saw them leave the stage. Akruti doesn't know that. She thinks I was 'stretching my legs' and this is what I told the police too. I needed to understand why they would leave stage suddenly like that during an important rehearsal.

The police and Akruti don't know much of the big picture. The entirety of what Brij suspects, which is also the reason I am here—and I cannot tell them yet. I will have to wait for Brij to do that. They don't even know about Brij, in fact— better left that way for now.

But the girls *really did* go to the restroom. It cannot have been them. It wasn't me. Nor was it Sanjna, after what she told us yesterday. *We're missing something.* I can feel it in my bones. The police will check the camera recording of that rehearsal. Zooming in step by step, maybe they will see what that is.

So, when I write 'all girls who left the stage', then at present I have no suspects. At least till the police re-examines the tape. I am almost certain that Lajjo was already stabbed before she began walking the ramp. Which is why the fact that the girls changed formation on ramp during the blackout doesn't matter so much. Though it was a disturbing diversion initially—it had never happened before. But then, no one had left stage in the blackout before either.

And Akruti's earlier observation also needs to be addressed: When Lajjo was stabbed, why didn't we hear her scream? Not just before she walked—even during her walk, or whenever it happened? When you are hurt, you cry out. Why didn't Lajjo?

So many unanswered questions, so many things awry here. Murphy's Law: Anything that can go wrong, will … and all at once too.

As of now, then—I'm at a standstill, perhaps till the police get the camera recording enhanced.

I am putting Nuzhat down as a possibility, but she couldn't have driven the knife in. We still need to find that person. Maybe an accomplice, if Nuzhat's the mastermind. But who? And, also: *why*?

My list of suspects for Doreen's murder

1. *The elusive Laddo.*

Now for this one, we have better progress. Having spoken to all who were with Doreen last—Inayat, Pia, Aishwarya, Sanjna, and Akruti—we can conclude there was one more person in the green room: this *Laddo*. Who may or may not have killed Doreen, but we still need her identity.

What about the girls we already spoke to, all these last ones? No perceived motive. None of them are serious contenders for the crown. None of them knew Doreen well, they haven't modelled previously. So why kill Doreen? Could one of them be the girl who bent the rules? They were in a group, and Doreen was a loudmouth, she would've let it out somehow. But she didn't. Which means *Laddo* couldn't be one of them. Besides, Akruti said she heard Doreen mention *Laddo* in the context of karma, i.e. she was the girl who bent the rules to be here. We really do need to find her.

2 p.m.

Lunch break. Which is truly unnecessary, because no one here looks like they're actually *eating*. If diet isn't causing a complete loss of appetite, the present circumstances we're caught in, certainly are. Two days to go to a contest finale, two unsolved murders and we're still cramming in two contest schedules. At least that means we're close to the end of this bizarre contest.

All the girls are wrung-out emotionally, big time. Every contest has some measure of stress I'm sure, but this year it's definitely on another level.

Tomorrow seems like a lighter schedule. It's just a day before the finale. Last minute sessions with our fitness mentor, Josy Joseph and the event head, Anjali Rodrigues. One rehearsal in the morning, then nothing ... just mental preparation for the contest the day after.

An awful situation to have to be living through, and nobody is leaving either. This can only end when the contest does. Unless somehow, *somehow*—we find the missing piece. *Laddo* ... where are you? *Who* are you?

3 p.m.

Lunch break done. But I've not been able to get the girls together or even a few of them, to ask about *Laddo*. They are so excitable. I really need this to happen. We have been told to go rest, reconvene at 5.30 p.m. for the talent round. Maybe we can talk to some of the girls then.

3:15 p.m.

In my room, roomie Tania's already asleep, her afternoon siesta time. I need time to think. I saw the morning's papers when we came up. Awful headlines, Akruti is in most of them. But what's interesting is that the papers haven't yet suggested the contest will be cancelled or postponed. It isn't even on the table, anywhere. So *Eye India* has been successful in feeding 'the show must go on' propaganda to all, the final pageant *will* happen.

There is speculation in the papers that there is a serial killer on the loose. That makes sense, it's most possible the two crimes were linked. But a serial killer killing just to spread fear and besmear the contest as the *Eye India* group is claiming to the media? To what end? No, there is more to this. We need to find that more. Do the papers know any additional information to what we do, right now? Doesn't seem so.

There is immense pressure on the police, the media has been reporting that too. But naturally. This is a national contest, with international ties. And an iconic one. 'The lives of all the other young contestants at stake,' one of the headline phrases used ... I only hope the Addl.CP manages to remain calm and not resort to hastiness in his investigation process.

Wonder if the man Akruti said she saw outside the window just now, is one of Mhatre's men? Her instincts are quite good, she felt he appeared suspicious. But she also seemed a bit overexcited in anticipation of the results of the swimsuit title, she knew they would be due this morning.

It is possible she could've just seen a lurking journalist. I made out as if not paying any attention to her, but I did make a mental note of her observation. Could this mystery man tie in at all with Brij's concern? We'll see how that plays out, it's wait-and-watch time. Strategy is required. Just like in our hunt for the mysterious *Laddo*.

The fact that we are all suspects is not written about overtly in the media either. Which is *Eye India*'s doing, keeping in mind that we do not want our Miss India 1995 to be a murder suspect should the killer not be found till the finale.

But we *must* find the person before that ... because if it is indeed a serial killer, as everyone is saying—*this person might kill again ...*

13

Akruti

'I WON, I did it!' All that was going on in my head the moment my name was announced as Miss India Perfect 10. For a moment I had doubted it, with everything being the way it was. But the swimsuit title came through, and with it intense relief for me. In all that was going wrong, this, at least, needed to go right. I wished Avi was around to share my joy and relief. But he was still not back, presumably still with the *Eye India* bosses, second day in a row. No doubt he would learn of my victory soon enough.

Parvati wanted me to help the police and I was happy to, but I also knew my goal. The reason for pressuring my parents and Jehaan to be able to continue here was clear to me, despite the mayhem—I wanted the crown, the same as when we began this contest. And winning this round helped me move a step closer to it.

Post the cheering and congratulatory photo-ops, and lunch, we were told to go back to our rooms. We had been instructed to gather downstairs at 5.30 p.m. The talent round was to begin at 6 p. m. When I reached the room, Roxanne was already asleep, she had wanted to rest before the evening's round. She was going to do a Bollywood dance.

Each of us had to perform, or reveal some talent we had. I was going to sing a song—it wasn't amazing but I had no intention of wasting my time on this particular round. It didn't count in terms of points towards the crown as much as the swimsuit round had. Nor would it really bring in any sort of positive publicity, since at present the media was all about the killings. I wanted now to conserve my mental and physical strength for the finale in two days. That evening's talent round would simply be a 'going through the motions' affair for me.

I knew Parvati would be reciting some poetry she had written herself. How like her to choose something so bookish as a talent. Not everyone understands poetry, and I would've advised her against it, had the round been important. But it really wasn't, so I let it rest.

In any case after what I had learned from Jehaan, I doubted she was actually here for a shot at the crown. *But why enter a Miss India contest if you don't want the crown?* My eyes shut as I pondered this. Next thing I knew Roxanne was shaking me awake as usual.

'We need to be down in fifteen minutes!' she semi-shouted. I smiled at her grumpy expression. Roxanne might appear to hate my guts, even prod me maliciously on occasion, but she had clapped the loudest when I won the swimsuit round. She knew she didn't have a chance in it, and I could tell she was genuinely happy for me, a person she knew closer than the others, as her roommate. I liked Roxanne's gruff, loyal, rambunctious attentiveness, so similar to my Jehaan's.

'On it,' I mumbled, sleepily, then as an afterthought, 'Do you happen to know any *Laddo* here, Roxanne?'

'Why would you ask that?' Roxanne looked at me, a trifle put out. 'Ten minutes to reporting time? Of course not! What is a *Laddo*? Are you talking of that Indian sweet?'

'Never mind,' I said to her, and proceeded to get ready at speed. By the time we had all gathered, this time in a makeshift green room near a huge stage constructed in the open air, it was nearing 6 p.m.

'Any luck?' Parvati found me immediately, I got the sense she had been waiting for me to arrive.

'Roxanne knows nothing about the name *Laddo*,' I said to her. 'Did you ask your roomie Tania?'

'She was asleep, and then got up and dashed to change—there was no time. But I will. Let's ask the rest when we can,' Parvati replied.

The area was swarming with police personnel. After the last two events, it was clear the Addl.CP and his team wanted to take no chances. Many media types were around too. I recognized a few familiar faces, but we were too far away for them to approach us, I was grateful for that.

There were around four-five minutes to go as we awaited the arrival of the judges. Parvati decided to tackle the pressing issue head first, there was no time to dilly-dally.

'Girls, there's a phone call outside for *Laddo* ...' she shouted out in the packed green room. That was the best way she could've asked about *Laddo*, under the circumstances, without appearing to be curious herself. All twenty contestants were present. Whoever *Laddo* was, she'd get up to take the call.

But to our surprise—no one did. There were a few curious stares, but the majority the girls were preoccupied, getting ready for their performances.

'What now?' I asked Parvati. She looked speculative, but we were out of time. Harried chaperones were directing us to different dressing tables.

The contest began. Roxanne started the proceedings, opening the event with a rousing Bollywood number. The music echoed around that huge stage. I clapped as hard as I could for her from backstage where we all stood. This round wasn't competitive for us, and besides I had genuinely enjoyed Roxanne's performance during rehearsals. She scored high too. Pia followed, with a Bharatnatyam performance, classic and touching.

Then there followed a display of immense physical strength from Vandana, which had us hooting in absolute amazement, backstage. Who would know she practised bodybuilding in her spare time? Lifting huge barbells whilst balancing precariously on one foot had the audience marvel at her muscles, as her control.

'Would you believe Vandana being able to do that?' I overheard Samantha whisper to Anuradha. 'How *powerful* she must be—wow!'

Nina was next. She was going to do a Bollywood item number apparently, one in which her idol SRK had also featured. It involved dancing on top of a moving train. Unfortunately, there was nothing she could use in terms of props that would move on stage as a train would.

So she improvised. Nina was to have a line of chairs up on stage, all placed at regular intervals with great gaps between them. She would show her dancing talent and her balancing and jumping skills as she danced on top of these, then leap from one chair to dance on the next, all on stage, in rapid succession.

This was not too dangerous in itself. But I think looking back now, Murphy's Law applied to every aspect of that contest in 1995. When she began, none of us noticed that the stage hands had placed one of the chairs too close to the edge of stage.

Nina's routine itself was flawless, luckily. You could tell she had practised and practised for it. She finished her performance with élan. But even as she dismounted from that final chair so close to the edge of stage, bereft of weight—it toppled over.

There were many from the audience right underneath that raised stage, there was no separating boundary. Someone would have been badly hit. But to our eternal awe and surprise, Nina, always so timid and afraid, deftly reached out and caught that falling chair, using her stocky, muscular build to bodily lift it safely back to stage.

Spontaneous claps erupted, both from the audience and from us backstage. We were all thrilled at her quick response, we had always believed Nina to be a bit on the slow side. We were also amazed at her strength, to have caught a heavy chair mid-fall and hosted it up back to stage, working against all that momentum, so fast! I think Nina clinched the Miss India Dream Talent title there and then with this masterful save, though we didn't know it as yet.

The next contestant, Samantha followed immediately, performing a comic skit she had written herself. The audience laughed appreciatively at her effort, the earlier scare forgotten.

Then Anuradha decided to wow the audience singing a contemporary ghazal number. There was a hushed silence at her sonorous voice. Followed by terrific applause. And the show went on.

I performed to a fair bit of applause, and even Parvati, despite her obscure choice of talent, I thought, managed to garner polite claps. The time came for Nuzhat to go on stage. The compere, on the mic announced her name. No reply. Again, the compere called for Nuzhat. Still she didn't appear.

'Nerves?' Roxanne whispered darkly to no one in particular, backstage. '*Nuzhat*? Never!'

We all knew what she meant. Nuzhat wasn't a nervous girl. Neither was she a popular girl, which was why, even after two announcements on stage no one was leaving to go search for her. The chaperones were running helter-skelter, as were the backstage personnel. Let them handle it, that was the mood among the contestants.

'HELP!' we heard Vandana call out just then. The panic in her voice had us all on our feet dashing towards the mobile restroom area adjacent to our green room. And there, once again, in a macabre replay of the past two incidents, we saw her.

Nuzhat lay immobile near the entrance to a restroom, her body bent at an angle, blood flowing from her head, which appeared bashed in. And near her, Vandana, holding the wall and Nessie both, for support, wouldn't stop screaming.

14
Akruti

Three successive murders at a Miss India Pageant—this was too much calamity even for Murphy's Law. The general air of hysteria ran rampant, spreading like wildfire from backstage to the audience. There was quite simply an uproar.

The police cordoned off the stage area almost immediately, even as event head Anjali Rodrigues rushed to the mic and declared as calmly as she could, that the talent round was over. The few contestants remaining would later be assessed privately by the judges, and Nina would be declared winner, but all of that seemed rather irrelevant in the awfulness of what had just transpired.

A frantic Vandana was being questioned by the expressionless Addl.CP Mhatre, and he was not going easy. This had happened on his watch, in full glare of the media and his bosses in the top rung of the Mumbai police force, who happened to be invited today. We gathered round her as Vandana sobbed.

'We were going to use the mobile restrooms, Nessie and I,' she explained to the Addl.CP between sobs. 'And we saw her Lying like that, not moving ...'

Vanessa, or Nessie, as all of us called her, interrupted. 'I checked for pulse. I would've called for Nina, as she has medical experience, but Vandana's screaming got everyone running to us immediately. Including the hotel doctor, who was here.'

'Did you see anyone else around?' the Addl.CP asked them.

'There was nobody. Not even in the restrooms, both stalls were empty. We were perhaps the first to discover her like that,' Nessie shuddered.

'Did you move the body at all?' the Addl.CP enquired, watching them closely.

'No,' Nessie answered, and Vandana nodded her compliance. 'I only checked to see if she had a pulse, but I didn't move her. Vandana didn't touch her at all.'

'Did you'll discover her together?' the Addl.CP asked.

'Yes,' Vandana said. 'We were both going to the restroom and met in the passage leading to it, so we walked to the mobile unit together. We saw her immediately.'

Nuzhat was no more. The doctor told us death had been instant when the skull had been smashed.

'Who was she with last, when alive?' this time the Addl.CP addressed us all.

Nobody spoke up. We all disliked Nuzhat intensely. But she was always around some of us, it wouldn't be that hard to recall who.

'… fight with her, where is she?' I heard a whisper behind me. Tania and Nina had their heads together speaking in low voices. But if I had heard them, so had everyone else. Including the Addl.CP.

'Speak up,' he turned to them. 'Who fought with whom?'

Tania and Nina exchanged surreptitious glances.

'Tara was with Nuzhat,' Tania's big, scared eyes looked into the Addl.CP's. 'She was telling her not to pick on her. I believe they had a bit of a scuffle. We heard them near the restrooms, when we were going in.'

'What did you hear?' the Addl.CP asked the two girls.

'Just a fight,' Tania said. 'Voices were indistinct, we couldn't make out the words. But we knew they were arguing, because they both sounded angry ...'

'Where is Tara?' the Addl.CP looked around. But she wasn't in the room. We were told to stay inside the green room, not disperse till the police had located Tara.

If the atmosphere in the past had seemed funereal at such gatherings, today it seemed positively sepulchral. The fact that one among us was missing was grave indeed. *Where was Tara?*

For an hour, we waited in that green room, in near-silence. Then, sounds of a scuffle and a heartbeat later, Tara, being led out, held by two women constables, weeping that it was not she who had killed Nuzhat.

I would not have thought that the cool and collected Parvati would react to this scene the way she did. But at the sight of Tara passing us, being dragged out by the two lady constables, she was up in a flash, blocking the entrance of the green room.

'Tell me Tara,' she said urgently, looking into the girl's eyes. To understand Parvati's intense reaction, it would perhaps help to go into Tara's personality. Tara was twenty-three, one of the oldest contestants in this pageant. Conversely, she also appeared to be the most naïve. This, despite the fact that she was a big city girl, as she kept explaining to anyone who would listen. We knew she wanted the crown dearly, not so much for the glamour of it but because she hoped it would do what she hadn't been able to do for very long ... attract lasting love from the right men.

Emotional and easily swayed, Tara had been at the receiving end of many of Nuzhat's taunts for her distinctive pigeon-toe'd style of walking all through our training these past weeks. She had pleaded, threatened and finally cried at the bullying, but to no avail.

Nuzhat had been relentless. Parvati had intervened on more than one occasion, asking Nuzhat to back off, telling Tara to calm down. Both girls somehow always heeded Parvati's words. She had that effect on people. Regardless, it was possible Nuzhat and Tara's scuffle earlier that day might be related to this on-going bad blood between them.

'Sit down, miss,' the surprised lady constable urged Parvati, even as a desperate Tara, freeing herself, violently caught hold of Parvati in a vice-like embrace. Her lips pushed close to Parvati's ears, she mumbled fierce words in the few seconds that elapsed before the constables managed to wrestle her away.

Parvati's face showed extreme emotion, but she was holding it in, like a mask. Her eyes searched the room, then rested on me. She came and stood behind me, whispering into my ear in a low tone.

'Tara says she hit Nuzhat, *but not hard enough to kill her,*' Parvati's voice was so soft, I strained to catch it. 'She was weak, but conscious and moving when Tara left to go on stage for her talent display. Tara's display was the one before Nuzhat's ...'

'Did *she* tell you this?' I asked Parvati, unbelieving at the turn of events. We both understood, without voicing it that Nuzhat was officially off our suspects list. How *could* she be? She was gruesomely hit and body bagged, and was now victim number three.

'In front of you just now,' came Parvati's low voice. 'Tara *did* have an argument with Nuzhat, which got heated because Nuzhat wouldn't stop troubling her and she was to be on stage in five minutes. She wanted mental peace before going on. In frustration, she hit Nuzhat, who fell down and pushed her head. Nuzhat appeared groggy after the blow. But she was sitting up when she left her, Tara said ...'

Before she could tell me more however, there was an announcement over the mic to the waiting media outside.

'We have in custody a suspect for the murder today. There will be an official statement this evening.'

I turned to face Parvati, meeting her sombre eyes. There was no doubt about it—innocent or not, Tara was going to be branded a murderer. The graver question loomed before us now—murderer *for how many murders?*

15

Akruti

'Meet me in my room now!' Parvati mouthed, even as our chaperones arrived to escort us back to our rooms. I nodded briefly to let her know to expect me soon, before heading upstairs.

One more sub-event had ended in tragedy. Would this be the end of the pageant, the final death blow? Everyone around us looked grim-faced and sombre. That there might indeed be a serial killer loose at the pageant was uppermost in people's minds.

I arrived in Parvati's room to find her alone. 'Tania's gone to Nina's room,' she told me. 'So we're free to talk.'

She had her diary open, and had already scribbled down some notes.

'What have you written?' I asked her curiously.

'A list of possible suspects, all the ones we've discussed so far. Till Doreen's murder, this only included our mysterious *Laddo*. Now there's yet another murder, and Tara's been thrown into the mix,' Parvati said, her voice grave. She did not mention Nuzhat on her list. There was no need.

No more did this entire scenario seem unreal. From the beginning we had felt this aura of unreality about all that was happening, and had allowed ourselves to be swept along, as events transpired. But now, even though Parvati and I, we had wanted to help the investigation, we were overcome by a very real sense of foreboding. It had existed before, but now it was sharp, a sense of clear and present danger.

The first murder had shocked us, me in particular, because it came out of the blue, and I was the one who caught Lajjo falling. The second had surprised and terrified us. Parvati had been particularly affected, because she discovered the body of Doreen. This third had simply knocked us sideways—even if the earlier two were not linked, three murders at the same pageant meant something extremely sinister and dark at play.

I could tell that not for a moment did Parvati believe that Tara was the murderer. *Did I?* Frankly, it was very confusing to me. If Tara indeed was a killer? Why did the police not hit upon it before? Why were the police not able to stop her committing her third crime right under their very eyes? *How had she pulled it off?*

These thoughts swirled in my head as I stared at Parvati scribbling in her diary.

'Do you know what else Tara told me in those few seconds she was near me?' she said finally lifting her head from the pages. 'She said she was told they believed she'd killed all three women. She said she was innocent. And I *believe her.*'

'Why?' I asked Parvati. 'Why do you believe anything she says?'

'Because there is *no motive.* Tara has no reason for killing Lajjo. She didn't know her well and she wasn't such a hot contender for this crown so as to be considered competition for Lajjo. She didn't leave the stage at all, she just shifted the formation when Smriti and Vanessa returned that night. And from the video recording, it appears that Lajjo was stabbed *before* she began to walk the ramp that night. In fact, Tara was standing almost at midpoint after the formation was shuffled. Lajjo had already been stabbed, *before* she reached Tara ...'

Parvati showed me the pages in her diary. She had written 'Lajjo' in red. Under which there was the word 'suspects'. Next to that, the word 'police' with a dash, and 'Tara'. Next to Tara's name in bold was written 'Motive' and a question mark.

'Tara had no motive for killing Doreen either,' Parvati continued. 'She only met Doreen at this pageant. She couldn't be the one who Doreen said had bent the rules because she could not *be Laddo*. Why do I say so? She had finished hair and make-up long before the rest, and did not enter the green room after.'

'How do you know this?' I asked softly.

'How do I know this?' Parvati's brown eyes fixed on mine solemnly. 'I was in the green room myself when Tara was getting ready, one of the first to do so, in fact. And she was next to me during the beginning of the swimsuit round, all through the first half, in fact. So I know she didn't leave during that window of time the police say Doreen was killed.'

I was amazed. It was lucky that Parvati was so observant of others, especially during the contest itself. Lucky for Tara that Parvati had noticed her movements during the swimsuit round and knew she wasn't *Laddo*. But how lucky was Tara, would her luck hold if the police named her culprit for all three killings?

'The reason Tara lunged at Nuzhat was self-defence,' said Parvati, writing this down, as she spoke to me. 'Remember, Nuzhat was constantly mean, maliciously bullying people, especially Tara. Today, Tara wanted peace before her stage appearance and Nuzhat wouldn't shut up. So Tara most probably lost control and went for her. More importantly, she said Nuzhat was alive after she hit her. So, whoever killed Nuzhat reached the scene *after* Tara left ...'

'Anyone could've killed Nuzhat,' I said slowly. 'She had made many enemies.'

'True,' Parvati said. 'But Akruti—think of each of us. Do any of us seem like we would *murder* someone to get back at them? If so, which of us seems the most vulnerable, the most likely to do so … in effect, impulsive and likely to commit a crime of passion?'

I knew exactly what she meant. If the police needed a scapegoat, they could not have found a better fall guy, a better victim than Tara. She was fragile, we all could see this. *Emotionally fragile, not physically so.*

She was the one, who had declared she had entered this contest to find love if she won. Not career success as the rest of us wanted, or to please boyfriends or seek stardom and fame. She *needed* to be loved. As a person, she seemed glaringly needy, obvious to anyone who came into contact with her, even briefly. And not strong-minded enough to deal with the likes of malicious Nuzhat. But could such a person, however fragile, be goaded into turning *this* violent?

'I honestly don't think it was her,' Parvati said to me. 'We really need to find this *Laddo*. And because I announced it to everybody today—she knows we're looking for her. Rather … *I'm looking for her.*'

The full import of Parvati's words hit me, chilling me to the bone. What she was saying was that if this elusive *Laddo* had indeed killed Doreen, she now knew Parvati knew of her existence. And she now also knew Parvati was looking for her.

If she had killed once or possibly repeatedly, what was to stop her from killing again? From killing those who she felt might know what she's done? Suddenly, it occurred to me— *Parvati might be the murderer's next target.* And by virtue or assumption of closeness—*so could I.*

One day to the finale …

16

Akruti

The Miss India Pageant 1995 would be continuing to its finale. Despite three murders, media frenzy, parents and loved ones up in arms, and a general air of unease and horror pervading everything, the show would go on. This was announced on the news the following day.

How the *Eye India* bosses managed to pull it off, swaying public opinion so, towards continuing with the contest, is anyone's guess. But today, three days after the first murder, the media stories were sympathetic to the pageant. I wondered if Avi, back on the premises now, after having spent two days with the *Eye India* bosses, had something to do with this turnaround in the press. His gift for reading nuances and turning them to one's advantage could only benefit the company, I thought wryly.

The broadcast media, while expressing horror and revulsion at the senselessness of 'young lives put out so terribly', had turned the idea of continuing the pageant into an issue of national pride. The newspapers too followed suit. *'Can we let this evil sabotage the way we live and work?'* one headline screamed, while another echoed the line *Eye India* had been repeating all this time: *'Despite everything, the show must go on.'*

The previous day had ended on a quiet note after our interlude in Parvati's room. As we discussed Tara and the grave importance of finding *Laddo*, Parvati's roomie Tania had returned. She expressed both interest and curiosity at Parvati scribbling so furiously in her diary. Taking this as our cue to end the discussion, I had excused myself and gone back to my room. No doubt Parvati had managed to fob off Tania's eager curiosity concerning her diary.

In my room, I called Jehaan.

'There was a stranger lurking outside in the garden, yesterday,' I told him, after the initial congratulations on my winning the swimsuit round were out of the way. Jehaan took my premiere placing in anything as a given. It was touching and perhaps even a little stressful to me at times, his absolute faith that I would best any challenge. Despite being at the top in his own line of work, he never failed to make a fuss about my victories, little or big. I loved that about him; loved how he both indulged and grounded me. But now I had other things on my mind.

'Dressed to look nondescript. And then, in the evening, Nuzhat was murdered. The police have taken Tara into custody, they were to make an announcement later,' I added.

'They did,' Jehaan brought me up to speed. 'They said they had a suspect, and that investigations were on. They hinted this person might be behind the other murders as well, they said interrogations were proceeding. They haven't named any names.'

So Tara has some time, I mused. How much, though?

'Do you really think it was this Tara girl? Do I tip off the news desk?' Jehaan was all business now.

'No, please don't Jehaan,' I implored. We shared an easy bond, expressing frank opinions on each other's professions.

But choices made in the pursuit of our individual career paths were our own. We were unerringly respectful of space and careful not to overstep there. By asking Jehaan to hold off, it might even appear that I was asking a professional favour of him. But I knew he trusted I had an important reason, trusted I wouldn't jeopardise his big story to follow my own agenda.

'Why? What else do you know, Aku?' Jehaan was all ears. 'Has Parvati told you something?'

'No, just my gut,' I had said to him. 'And yes, Parvati's conviction, that it wasn't Tara. Tara's the fragile sort. Easy scapegoat for the police.'

'Wouldn't be the first time,' Jehaan had said grimly. 'There's tremendous pressure on them to find the culprit.'

Jehaan had no other information to share and presently I had rung off. Like after Doreen's murder, my sleep had been uneasy, at first. My roomie Roxanne had come up while I was in bed; she had been in another contestant's room all this while. I heard her come in, my mind restless. But soon the exhaustion took over, and I slept, waking up only the next morning to the day's headlines, telling us the contest would still be a go.

'Looks like you'll get your shot at the 1995 crown, after all,' Roxanne had flung me a cheeky glance listening to the television commentary.

I was grateful for her ribbing, everything else at the pageant had acquired ghoulish and morbid proportions, affecting our mood and morale both.

'Get ready, Roxanne,' I told her, almost affectionately. 'Today we have to meet Mr Joseph for the final time. Hope you've worked on your abs!' Mentor sessions had all but wound up, yesterday was Lubaina Pervez's final one, today would be the fitness mentor, Josy Joseph's. Abdominal crunches were Roxanne's undoing, she really hated them.

'My abs are just fine,' Roxanne sniffed at me. 'It's my mind that needs pampering.'

I met her eyes, and there was understanding there. It was a strange, tumultuous time, horrific days, restless nights. Candy floss contests and relentless cruelty do not pair well. But we were all in it together, and that counted for something.

'I think Anjali might have a word with us about tomorrow,' Roxanne said, before moving off to get ready. Anjali Rodrigues was the event head for the *entire* proceedings. No matter what had transpired up until now, we knew she wanted to ensure that tomorrow worked like clockwork. Just as we did.

As Roxanne took her time in the bathroom getting ready, there was a brief knock on the door. I opened it, thinking it might be our chaperone, telling us to hurry up. The fitness session was always early, and this one was to be followed by one final rehearsal for tomorrow. Then Anjali would address us. The evening was free, in preparation for the finale tomorrow.

But it wasn't the chaperone. It was Parvati, looking troubled.

'Akruti, did you take my diary with you when you left yesterday?' she asked quietly.

'No,' I said. 'Remember, you were still shutting it when I let myself out? You'd told Tania it was nothing private, but that you didn't want to show her your lopey handwriting?'

'Did I?' Parvati looked disturbed. 'I can't seem to find it. Maybe the stress is getting to me. I'll search again. Thanks, Akruti.'

'Sure. I hope you find it,' I told her, shutting the door again. There was no time for small talk. By now, we understood each other well; knew when to be brief and business-like.

Parvati had left to go search her room again. Though she was ready, I knew she wouldn't be going downstairs immediately. Not unless she found her diary. I could tell she was upset. After all, her diary contained all our queries, guesstimates and surmises on the murders till now. Also— our suspicions about the elusive *Laddo*.

While our efforts would seem amateurish to more experienced investigators, in the wrong hands, especially those of an unhinged serial killer, the diary would be dynamite. Not so much because of the conclusions or guesses Parvati had jotted so far, but for the fact that it showed clearly and without doubt that *we*—both Parvati and I—*were intent on finding out the killer's identity.* That itself would put us in grave danger, perhaps enough to make us both targets ourselves.

Now, writing this with the hindsight and maturity that comes with age, I wonder how we were not absolutely panicked at this development. But so much had happened by then that losing a diary, even an important one, seemed tame by comparison. There was already enough darkness around. I think we simply thought that the diary would turn up, sooner or later.

We met just a little while after, in Josy Joseph's final fitness session. All of us in shorts or tights or tracks, equipped for demonstrations if he needed.

'Hydrate yourself well,' Joseph bellowed; a small man with a big presence. 'Remember—your mind is already under pressure on the big day. No need to add pressure to your body as well. *Stay in the zone!*'

This line was his favourite, and spontaneously, we all broke into cheers as he spoke. This was after all, his final session with us, and his presence, basic, sunshiny and strong, brought us all back to why we were actually here. He suddenly made us believe in the reality of the competition, rather than the reality of terror and death that had gripped us these past days.

'This is your moment, ladies,' he was saying. 'The moment you all have been intensely training for, all these days and weeks past. *Give it everything!'*

As we all sat, attentive and adoring, listening to Joseph's fitness tips for the big day following this one, my eyes sought Parvati. They wandered to her face but she seemed distracted and did not look at me even once, throughout the session.

'Use your muscles!' Joseph was saying, then to giggles, '*Not* just the ones in your head!' He flexed his own, taut and ropey, and I suddenly had a random thought. Joseph was so strong—and Nuzhat's killer had bashed her head in, with immense strength. Even the blade that killed Lajjo had been driven in with great force. What if it wasn't a contestant, but a *mentor* who had killed both?

Joseph was both popular and efficient at his work, besides his vibe was sunny and forward looking, there was no doubt about it. But who said a killer needed to appear sulky and dour-faced? By that logic, the Addl.CP with his taciturn expression and exacting nature would be the first in line for the title, only he was a policeman, not a murderer!

Joseph's was a short, snappy, lively session, just like the man, and it ended quickly to thunderous applause. If Joseph had succeeded in one thing, it was to reawaken in us all, competitive fire for the finale. His bright, just-do-it demeanour had also lifted a little, the all-pervasive cloud of gloom we had been struggling under.

There was a quick break before our final stage rehearsal and I rose from my seat, determined to speak to Parvati about my sudden epiphany. To my chagrin, she wasn't in the room. I couldn't locate her in the restrooms nearby either.

I was just about to give up, when I saw her enter the rehearsal hall where we were to begin our final sequence.

'Where have you been?' I hissed at her as the music commenced and we all scurried up to ramp, making a quick dash to wear our high heels before final run through. No more dress rehearsals—this was to be a fairly fast affair, just to have us prepared and ready for the finale the next day.

'Trying to find my diary,' Parvati mouthed. 'It was definitely *taken*, Akruti.' And then, as the chill ran up my spine, she added, '*Someone read it.*'

17

Akruti

The whole rehearsal passed in a blur. I couldn't wait for it to get over fast enough so I could reach Parvati and ask her about what she said to me.

Finally it was done, and we broke for lunch before Anjali, the event head, could have a final word with everyone.

I walked up to Parvati, grabbed her arm. What a role reversal! Four days ago, she had grabbed mine after Lajjo's stabbing, and I had been the reluctant one.

'I have it now,' Parvati understood my impatience, and appeared to be expecting it. She added calmly enough, 'My diary. *But it went missing the entire morning.*'

'What do you mean?' I asked, afraid of both her calmness and what she was implying.

'I was unsure,' Parvati's tranquil mood seemed to harden as she spoke fiercely. 'I thought I was suffering from stress, I had misplaced it. I turned everything upside down looking for it. And when I couldn't find it, I finally gave up and came down for Josy's session.'

'Go on,' I said, watching her intently.

'But I couldn't stop thinking about it, so I went back up in the break to look for it again,' she continued.

'So that's where you were,' I interrupted. 'I was looking for you!'

'Akruti—the diary was in my room, in my drawer when I went back up. *Locked.*' Parvati pressed on. 'It wasn't there during my frantic search all morning. *But it was there on my return,*' she emphasized. 'Someone took it. And replaced it, thinking I wouldn't miss it.'

'Tania, your roommate?' I asked, horrified.

'I wouldn't know,' Parvati said. 'Tania left the room very early, I wasn't even awake then. She came down to Josy's session without returning to the room. She didn't see my frantic search for it.'

'She seemed very eager to know what was in there yesterday,' I mused. 'But Parvati—your drawer was *locked.*'

'Yes,' Parvati nodded. '*Before* and *later*, when I found it. Someone has obviously gotten a key or has made one, because mine is always with me. This person made me think I was losing my mind ...'

Parvati's shoulders shook, I realized with a start just how heavy a toll the incident had taken on her. Impulsively, I gave her a sudden hug, but she stepped back awkwardly, surprised at my gesture.

'I thought it was stress, that I hadn't been careful enough,' Parvati met my gaze, the corners of her eyes deceptively watery. 'I was so distraught. But then I realized how particular I *always* am,' she said, her chin suddenly up, shoulders square.

'I realized I *wasn't* mistaken, I *hadn't* lost it, someone *took* it,' she added, her voice trembling.

I realized with a start that Parvati was crying ,,, with rage!

'This person made me second guess *myself*,' Parvati was saying, voice low but steely. 'I won't let it happen again.'

'Have you asked Tania?' I asked.

'If she is the culprit, she has no clue I knew it was gone,' Parvati said. 'She wasn't in the room when I searched. Nor when I came to ask you if you had it. I prefer her or whoever it is, to think I don't know they had it. We work from there,' she said.

'But certainly, she seems to be the only one who could've had access,' she further mused. 'Didn't seem like a thief, though.'

'If she was just curious, it's still okay,' I said. 'She'd have read it and that's all. But if it wasn't her … if it were someone else, *someone who is also a killer …*'

'And who's to say Tania won't talk or share what she's read?' Parvati countered. 'She or whoever did it. Either way, we have to assume that their intentions were harmful.'

When Parvati spoke like this, it brought to my mind that she had grown up watching her RAW agent dad at work, possibly imbibed some tricks.

'So you're saying we're in danger?' I asked.

'I'm saying we need to make sure we aren't caught out in the same situation, twice,' Parvati looked at me, suddenly smiling to break the tension. 'You keep my diary now, Akruti.'

'Oh-hh. Okay,' I said, a trifle nonplussed.

'What did you want me for, earlier?' Parvati asked, suddenly changing the topic.

'To discuss whether a mentor could've killed Lajjo and Nuzhat,' I told her. 'I was watching Josy earlier, it came to me then. He is so strong. And it was a person of great strength who hit Nuzhat and stabbed Lajjo.'

'It could be anybody,' Parvati said. 'Not just a mentor. The part about the strength, I do agree with. Only a very strong person could do this. But what motive could Josy possibly have to kill them? And if Doreen's murder is linked, Josy wasn't even there. Nor could he be *Laddo*, he has no hair!'

I smiled at her attempt at levity, but also, I was stumped—it was true, all she said.

'Could either Vandana or Nessie have done it?' I asked. 'They found Nuzhat, remember?'

'It's like saying could either you or me have done it,' Parvati spoke wryly. 'You held Lajjo as she toppled. I found Doreen, along with Tania. But even if it were a serious question—what motive? Neither Nessie nor Vandana were really the butt of Nuzhat's malice. And neither of them could be *Laddo*—they had finished hair and make-up early at the swimsuit round.'

I marvelled at Parvati's power of observation again. She saw so much, without appearing to. I was known for my own retentive ability in modelling circles, but somehow at this contest, I found myself lacking. I had been in a position to notice things on two occasions, with both Lajjo and Doreen and yet managed not to. Sharp as I might seem, I had much to learn from Parvati, I decided.

It was time for us to go to the final session of the day, that led by event head Anjali Rodrigues.

'Let's speak after Anjali's talk,' Parvati said to me. 'It is crucial we find *Laddo*.'

I nodded, following her into the room. Just as we were to be seated, she turned, looking at me.

'By the way, Akruti, to answer your earlier question ...,' Parvati said softly. 'We were *always* in danger. You, when you publically clutched at a murder victim who was also your arch-rival. And I, when I announced there was a phone call for *Laddo—and no one came forward* ...'

18

From the pages of Parvati's Diary

2 p.m.

The final session. I find this SO BORING, but we have to get through it. I'm writing as event head Anjali Rodrigues speaks. I like her hair though, so individualistic, that electric blue!

She's going on about how we are in the midst of a huge crisis, but our characters will be stronger for it if we keep our heads down and concentrate on why we are all here. No other contest has attracted this kind of publicity. But then few other contestants would be as pressured as we have been over the last few days. Unusual times call for unusual measures, she's telling us. And unusual courage to continue with our dreams, despite all. A remarkable pep talk, I have to say.

As Miss India contests go, this year is surely one from hell for everybody behind the scenes. And for all those competing of course. But listening to Anjali brings everyone some comfort, we need it, definitely.

3 p.m.

Anjali's speech is over, I like how she kept it short and sweet. Fiery lady, audacious too in her comments about ignoring other people's agendas and concentrating on your own. The police wouldn't be too thrilled. Though she didn't mention anyone in particular, we all understood her.

We are to forget we were suspects in two murders and simply think about the crown. Anjali's cool-headedness is admirable, but so much is resting on her ability to pull this off without glitches tomorrow.

I would actually look upon *her* as a possible suspect for this very cool-headedness! But what could she gain by making the contest go awry? Her reputation depends on it running smoothly! So strike Anjali from suspect list, I guess. Unless a bigger angle appears ... like the one Brij was referring to. But for that I need assistance, so I won't count that in yet.

3.30 p.m.

We have the rest of the day free. Time enough to figure out who *Laddo* is. Time enough to try and find out why my diary was taken. And yet ... not enough time to save Tara from incriminating herself?

6 p.m.

Akruti and I, we've been sitting together for the last few hours in Akruti's room, trying to clear our heads about what's been happening. Roxanne isn't here so it's private enough for now. We certainly can't meet in my room now, not after the missing diary incident—it would be foolhardy. Anyway, as to our effort so far: we've decided to take it step by step, go over each murder and scene of crime.

So, about Lajjo's murder: we assumed Lajjo was stabbed *before* she walked the ramp, looking at the video recording. She was already stumbling, pre-empting the music, possibly befuddled from acute blood loss, though nobody realized it then. *But Lajjo didn't leave the stage at all.*

So whoever did it had to be stationed either at the very far end of the stage where Lajjo was waiting, or have come in and slipped out in record time in the thirty-second blackout.

Going over the last few girls who were next to Lajjo or could've moved to stab her, there are Smriti and Nessie, of course, who left the stage and messed up the formation. There is me obviously, who could be regarded as suspect for the same reason. And then there is Nina who was closest to her during the blackout, but who never left stage at all.

The dilemma being, Lajjo was standing last, the girls were all *in front* of her. So, if we go with the theory that she was stabbed *before* she walked—*it discounts everyone on stage automatically*, whether or not they shuffled position. Which leaves the three of us, who left the stage and I know no one did it. I followed the girls to the restroom and back … so *how* do we tackle this?

'What if we assume that Lajjo was *not* stabbed earlier?' Akruti says.

But she was walking unsteadily from the very beginning, I tell her … unless she was walking that way *not* because she was stabbed, but *because she had been drugged …*

We were suddenly energised by this surmise—how else to explain an inexplicable dilemma?

We need to find the Addl.CP to confirm it, the post mortem would tell us if indeed she was *also* administered something. Which would change how we viewed the murder, change our list of suspects—change everything, in fact …

'Take for a moment that Lajjo *was* stabbed *on* stage,' I muse. 'Whose costume would be such that a blade could be hidden in its folds? One so sleek and elegant, but one where such an instrument could be made easily accessible when needed?'

This was an angle we hadn't even thought to ponder on earlier. I wonder if the police had.

'It would have to be one of the girls standing at the very beginning of ramp,' Akruti says. 'Because even with this theory, that she was stabbed *on* stage, it would have had to have been in the thirty-second blackout—in the mayhem of the girls shuffling and shifting position to accommodate the sudden presence of Smriti and Vanessa, returning to stage …'

We had all been in gowns, but each gown was cut differently, and many were revealing, to ensure our figures were on display. It would have been difficult to hide a blade in many of them. But not all. So, *which of us could've tried?*

As we got ready to list the girls in their gowns, there was a knock on the door.

'You've been summoned,' Akruti's chaperone popped her head in as the door opened, looking at us both. 'By the police.'

19

Akruti

Everything it seemed, was coming to a head all at once. There was intense anticipation in the air now, and it wasn't only because the long-awaited finale would be held the next day.

'The Addl.CP wants you in the interrogation room downstairs,' my chaperone had arrived unexpectedly to tell me. She seemed unsurprised to see Parvati with me. 'You, as well.'

'Thank you, Sheila,' I said to her, as we headed down. I felt a bit sorry for all the contest chaperones. Like in most pageants, they had been chosen from the mainly lifestyle sections of the vast *Eye India* employee pool, to supervise and tend to the contestants' needs. But the job, entailing constant running around, and carry-fetch situations, could get tiresome on long days. At the 1995 contest, it would've been positively dismal. Not just because of some of the petulant demands of the nervy girls, but because the *Eye India* bosses no doubt felt they could've managed their charges better—not allowed for such catastrophes to descend at all, as they had, one after another.

Right now however, the plight of the chaperones was farthest from anyone's mind. We both made haste to meet the Addl.CP, we believed he might have need of us at this point.

As we entered the room, we realized that our guess had been right.

'I need you to identify someone,' Addl.CP Mhatre launched into the reason for our summons, without pleasantries, the moment he saw us. 'We have attempted to go over the tape recording the night Lajwanti Khan was stabbed, moment by moment. We could not see this part till we zoomed in.'

He had already switched on the recording on the monitor beside him. We saw a blurry enlarged close-up of the beginning of ramp, close to the stage. It was in darkness, shot during the thirty-second black-out, and figures were in shadow, indistinct.

We saw the formation shift as Smriti and Vanessa scrambled back to ramp from their restroom visit. As the girls moved, the Addl.CP froze the frame, then pointed to a corner, deep in the shadows, almost in the wings, where the ramp met the stage. A figure, partially hidden by the curtain but visible on stage, was revealed. The person appeared not short, but not as tall as the rest of the contestants. As the Addl. CP advanced the recording frame-by-frame in slow motion, the figure moved behind the wings and then was gone.

'Who is this?' Addl.CP Mhatre asked us.

We were shell-shocked. The figure could not be a sound and light or stage technician. They had strict instructions never to step out of the wings or be seen, even in darkness. Nor could it be backstage help, for the same reasons

It wasn't one of us obviously, there was no hesitation or haste in the movements of this person, no scrambling to be *on* ramp before the lights came on. We were unsure as to whether it was a man or a woman, because it was all in darkness, only a frontal silhouette was seen.

Not in heels, so definitely not one of us. In fact, even in the small time-frame the figure appeared, the person seemed confident of their movement—this was no restless event representative, shifting in and out of the wings, revealed by mistake. The shadow was deliberately there, half-hidden, but watching the ramp, then slipping away. Watching ... *what*?

'We have no idea,' I told the Addl.CP, even as Parvati nodded her ignorance.

'Does this mean your suspect for Lajjo's murder is *not* one of the contestants?' Parvati asked quietly, then added deliberately, 'Therefore ... *not* Tara?'

I was alarmed at her forwardness. This was, after all, an on-going investigation, and to all extents and purposes, Tara had been taken into custody, though not officially named as a suspect.

'This means we need to look for this person,' the Addl. CP's reply revealed nothing. He did not seem to have been offended by Parvati's bold query, but he wasn't revealing anything further either.

'I'm disappointed you do not know who this shadow form could be,' he added. Then, addressing Parvati only, he said, 'Especially since you had stepped out of the ramp formation too. What was it you said you had needed to do ... 'stretch your legs?'

'I do not know who this person could be,' Parvati met his eyes squarely, as was her habit. She did not rise to his bait either, the one underlining the fact that she had changed formation as well, to 'stretch her legs' as she'd insisted.

'Did you get a post-mortem done on Lajjo, Addl.CP?' Parvati pressed on with her concern, her eyes serious.

'Yes,' Mhatre was observing her keenly. 'What is it that you are getting at?'

'Was there some uncommon substance in her system?' Parvati asked gravely. 'Drugs, or something like that?'

The Addl.CP's eyes narrowed. 'Is there something you know that you want to tell us?'

'What if she wasn't stabbed *before* she walked the ramp, as we thought when we saw the tape first?' Parvati stated. 'What if she was *drugged first*, so she was not herself, not in touch with reality ... and *then* stabbed, very much *on* ramp? Remember, she had already begun walking, pre-empted the music cue before the lights even came on ... so in actuality, she was walking, *passing each of the girls on ramp in darkness* for the first few minutes. Time enough to drive a knife in ...'

'The tape doesn't show much,' the Addl.CP's eyes were speculative. 'In fact. it's all a blur at the back of ramp in that blackout, a confusion of dark shadows as the girls scramble to shift into position. It's a wonder we managed to get that silhouette I asked you about ...'

Then, as if coming to a decision, he said, 'It *is* possible. We *did* find a substance. But we weren't paying much attention to it. It was a psychotropic drug. The kind that would no doubt, make a person very sleepy. We assumed it was a leftover from medication she was under, to calm herself before the finale. We understand she was suffering from extreme stress.'

Parvati's eyes looked jubilant. 'You *know* Tara could not have done this,' she told the Addl.CP. 'You *know* this.'

'I will not discuss any suspects at this point,' Mhatre was being his maddeningly aloof self. 'It would help Tara, though, if you managed to think of who this person so silhouetted could be ...'

Mhatre had all but dismissed us, but I had one more thing on my mind.

'About the Doreen case ...,' I was silent all this while, but had to ask. After all this was Parvati's pet project. 'Who is *Laddo*, Addl.CP? Did you find out?'

'Not yet,' the Addl.CP's reply was curt, as if he was done with us for the time being.

'*She may well be the killer*,' I spoke out, emboldened by Parvati's earlier frankness.

The Addl.CP didn't reply, but we knew he had heard and noted the comment. Our interview was done, we let ourselves out.

'We *must* find this *Laddo*,' Parvati said, as we walked out of the room, to head back upstairs. 'The police are chasing different leads, we *must* follow ours ...'

'Yes,' I told her, disturbed, as I put the diary she offered me in my handbag. 'We don't have time, though. Nor anything to go upon ...'

'It will turn up,' Parvati mused, cutting me off, before I could complete my sentence. 'The clue. We need to go over each murder over and over again, till it does ...'

20

Akruti

'All prepared for tomorrow, girls?' Josy Joseph's booming voice suddenly penetrated our consciousness and conversation. So engrossed were we in our discussion that we had not noticed him in the passage leading to the elevators. With him walked our speech mentor, the self-possessed Lubaina Pervez.

'As prepared as we'll ever be,' I said, confidently. I was, after all, expected to do well in this contest. It didn't seem right to appear diffident now.

'That's the spirit!' Josy said robustly, even as Lubaina watched us in speculation.

'Were you called in by the police just now?' she asked. 'Is there progress on this situation?'

'No idea,' Parvati spoke up. 'We aren't being told anything.'

'Are you both nervous at all?' Josy was asking.

'Well, it would be foolish to say we aren't,' I told him. 'It's the finale after all …'

'Do the meditation I taught you,' Josy said decisively. 'The power of it is such you feel better immediately. Do it tonight. In fact, do it right now!'

I smiled at him, thinking he wasn't serious, but to our surprise, he was.

'Both of you! Show me how you do it,' Josy said.

We couldn't very well refuse our mentor, especially the popular one who had been coaching us for the better part of two and a half weeks.

'You can do it standing up. Get rid of inessentials first. Physically—'

'Here, let me take your things,' Lubaina said hastily, reaching for both our handbags, unsurprised at this impromptu relaxation lesson. She had worked with Josy on this pageant for the past many years, was no doubt used to his take-charge ways.

'—then mentally. Now close your eyes. Breathe …' Josy instructed.

Nonplussed, we did as we were told. The meditation was to be in silence, counting breaths in intervals of ten. We did this silently, our eyes closed as Josy counted for us.

It was done in five minutes, but five minutes of inactivity can be a long time for minds in hyper-mode. I don't know if we were able to wind down as much as Josy wanted us to, but we assured him we felt much more relaxed and he looked pleased.

'Have you seen that girl, Shilpi?' Lubaina asked us as we thanked Josy.

'You mean Nina,' I said, instantly.

'Yes, of course,' a faint line of annoyance crossed Lubaina's face, but her brow fell back into smooth lines almost immediately. 'I meant Nina. Have you seen her?'

'No, we haven't,' Parvati told her. 'Do you want us to fetch her?'

'No, that's all right,' Lubaina said, checking her watch— our cue to exit, definitely.

We claimed our bags from Lubaina who bade us a snappy good luck—she wasn't one for unnecessary casual conversation out of turn, as Josy was. Her air was aloof, her pep talks reserved for her sessions alone.

'Well, that was an unexpected encounter,' I said to Parvati as we waited to hail the elevator to head to our rooms upstairs.

Parvati didn't answer, she just looked speculative, lost in thought. As she was being uncommunicative, my gaze wandered to the lobby, visible from the elevator area.

And I started, because all of a sudden, I saw the same person I had seen on the lawn outside during Lubaina's session. The man purposely dressed so as to appear nondescript, at a distance still, but nearing us now. He was walking rapidly down the lobby area coming straight to the elevators. *Coming straight to us.*

'Parvati, *look,*' I urged, turning violently to get her attention, because she was behind me. She stepped forward, but he had moved like lightning it seemed. He had entered an adjoining lift a short distance from us in that split second and the door shut unceremoniously in our faces as we raced up the stairs.

'It was that man I saw!' I told her urgently. 'The man you felt might be a journalist. But Parvati—no journalists are allowed in this area now. *And he's used the restricted access elevator.'*

Parvati looked at me, her eyes hooded. 'Maybe he was a plains-clothed policeman. We should concentrate on what *we* want to find, leave the uncertain parts of the jigsaw to the experts ...'

'What if no one from this contest is a murderer?' I persisted. 'What if it's a complete outsider, like this person? And we're not even telling the Addl.CP ...'

'Tell Mhatre you saw him, if you must,' Parvati said curtly. 'Either you'll be telling him of the existence of one of his own men or it might be new information ... But, Akruti—Mhatre isn't going to share anything important with you regardless. He didn't earlier, did he? Better we concentrate on how we can best help Tara for now, don't you think?'

'If she's innocent, that is,' I said brusquely. I wasn't happy about Parvati brushing off this person just like that. And nerves for next day were also a factor, if I was being honest about it. I *really* wanted this crown.

'Oh, she is,' Parvati said gently. She was intuitive, guessed I was a bit cheesed off right then.

She continued, 'Shall we continue our methodical listing of the events so far? To try and search for something we might have overlooked or missed? It would keep your mind off the finale tomorrow. Unless you'd rather just de-stress in your room?'

'No, I want to do this with you,' I said.

She was right, it was better for me to divert my mind from the finale. I wanted it too bad to be calm just then. Occupation with something else would help. And this something else was far bigger than the contest—darker, joyless. But I'd never been one to shy away from reality.

'Give me my diary,' Parvati said as we finally entered the elevator to go up. 'We'll need to write down all we discuss once again.'

I opened my bag to hand her the book. Only I couldn't find it.

'Parvati …' I looked up, suddenly fearful. '*It's not here …*'

21

Akruti

'Don't be silly,' Parvati met my eyes with the cool-headedness that was so typical of her. 'It has to be. Maybe you put it in a different compartment of your bag. Search again.'

Sure enough, it was as she said. There was the diary, in the second compartment. I pulled it out, shuddering in relief.

'Thought I'd lost it,' I said, handing it to her.

We stepped out of the elevator, to go back to my room.

With unending good fortune, we realized Roxanne hadn't yet returned. We had the room to ourselves.

I put coffee to brew in the coffee maker—if we were going to be brainstorming for a bit we needed a strong fix to keep us going.

Parvati began flipping the pages of her diary absentmindedly, as she waited for my attention.

'You remind me of me,' I said, catching her eye in the mirror in front of the coffee maker.

'I do?' Parvati looked puzzled.

'Yes. Your expression—lost in thought,' I explained to her. 'I felt the same, I remember, while Doreen was doing my hair. She wouldn't stop chattering … and I caught the time on the clock in the mirror facing me, just like I'm catching your eye now … and I only wanted her to finish, so I could go!'

'She was being her usual self, telling me about her husband, his Dubai job, I was distracted, only half listening. Just as you now, lost in thought—only my thoughts were on the imminent swimsuit round,' I continued. 'But she was a well-meaning soul, y'know, for all her chatter. She was basically conveying her husband's good will to me. He told her I was his favourite, even though he'd worked with three people in the contest before, Doreen told me. That was so sweet, I felt so bad later—'

'Repeat that,' Parvati has sat up straight cutting my prattle abruptly.

'Repeat what?' I asked, startled at her sudden brusqueness.

'What you just said,' Parvati's voice was low, expectant.

'... That Doreen told me I was her husband's favourite in the contest?' I asked astonished.

'No, after that,' Parvati's voice had turned low and silky, that special voice she used when she knew she was onto something important.

'That I was his favourite despite the fact that he'd worked with three contestants before?' I asked, now completely at sea. 'What's the big deal, Parvati?'

'The deal, Akruti,' Parvati's voice was thick, predatory. 'Is that Doreen's husband is a make-up artist. He works only with professional models. *But you and Lajjo were the only two professional models in the contest. So who was the third contestant Doreen's husband was supposed to have worked with?*'

I gazed at Parvati open-mouthed. That she could've found something of such significance in a half-remembered conversation, narrated as prattle rather than a serious attempt at fact-finding—I was overcome with something akin to awe.

'Oh my God!' I mouthed. 'I can't believe I remembered this only now. It's important, *so* important ...'

'You are sure she said he'd *worked* with three people in this contest? Not 'known' them, because that could imply a general relationship, not a professional one?' Parvati quizzed me.

'Yes,' I told her. 'Even though I was listening absent-mindedly, my powers of retention as you know are fair ...'

'More than fair,' said Parvati, looking at me with gratitude. Then her expression turned serious once more.

'Someone else in this contest had modelled professionally. Someone who hid that fact for professional or other reasons. *Why*?' Parvati was writing the very words she was speaking aloud to me, in her diary.

'Could this person be ashamed of the kind of modelling she's done?' I offered. But even to me that didn't ring right. Any professional experience gave one confidence, any publicity was good publicity in the modelling line.

'Perhaps. Or then ... this person bent the rules to be here. No one knew ... *but Doreen must have,* she said so. And she must have, not because this contestant told her, but because her husband told her ... he had *worked* with this person.' Parvati continued.

'*The elusive Laddo!*' I breathed in sudden realisation. 'The third contestant was *Laddo!*'

Parvati met my eyes then, looking up from her precious diary.

'Possibly, yes,' she acquiesced. 'And both Doreen and her husband knew the contestant fairly well, because they used a pet name no one here is familiar with.'

'And *no one* in this contest seems to know who *Laddo* is ...' I added.

'Either that ... or we haven't been persistent enough,' Parvati said grimly. '*Someone* does. And we need to find them.'

'You know who might have a clue?' I suddenly had a brainwave. '*Avi*! He has worked with everyone. Even if he hasn't, his gossip network is legendary. He wasn't in the green room when you shouted out about that phone call for *Laddo,* hoping to find out her identity. He has no clue we're even doing this, or looking for her ... *but he might know her.*'

'It is best not too many know that we're investigating,' Parvati's eyes were hooded again. She thought for a moment, then appeared to have come to a decision.

'But we can always ask Avi casually,' she said. 'In fact, better if *you* do it, Akruti. You know him best. Do it casually, so he doesn't suspect anything.'

Roxanne entered the room before we could even get down to discussing the other murders. We were running out of time, both of us were acutely conscious of the fact. We greeted Roxanne, and she shot us a curious glance before heading to the restroom.

'See you later,' Parvati's eyes warned me to stay silent as she got up and made to leave. 'Rest well for tomorrow.'

'There is still the morning,' I told her brightly.

'Don't put off for tomorrow what can be done today,' Parvati mouthed the age-old homily lightly, but I knew what she meant. Parvati knew she was onto something, she meant for us to move in quickly before the track went cold. That the contest was on the morrow mattered little to her in actuality.

Also, it seemed to me, we were working out quite a code in front of others. But would it lead to something, all this effort on the eve of what was most important to *my* career at least? Shouldn't I actually be resting up for the big night to come?

I knew I had to try and do both to the best of my ability. My conscience would not allow me to stop helping Parvati, even if my ego would not take a defeat at the contest kindly.

I decided I would call Avi once Roxanne went down for dinner. I needed privacy.

'Your bag is open,' Roxanne said, as she flopped down on her bed returning from the restroom.

With a start I realized I had forgotten to shut it earlier, rummaging about for Parvati's diary. And I realized in her hurry, Parvati had taken her diary with her, back to her room. The very room where it went missing for a bit. I made a mental note to call her once Roxanne left the room.

As I shut my bag, a notion, and then the surety of it came to me. I had put Parvati's diary in a different compartment from the one I finally found it in. But my bag had been with me all along—so how then had it travelled to the second compartment from the first?

'The mystery of the missing diary is nothing in comparison to the mystery of the missing *Laddo*,' I said to myself, giving my head a little shake in an effort to clear it. 'I'll ponder over this one later. Let me get down to calling Avi first.'

22

Akruti

⌒

'*Aku!*' Avi's voice was both firm and breathless. Only Avi could sound this way. I had called him the instant Roxanne went down for dinner. She had cajoled and coaxed and finally threatened me to go with her to eat, but I had insisted that I wasn't hungry.

'Fine—you might want to look ultra-thin by starving yourself for the big finale tomorrow, but remember, fainting for lack of adequate food intake is not an option!' she had sniffed in defeat and flounced off.

I had nodded indulgently at her. No matter how sarcastic Roxanne was, her kind-heartedness always shone through.

'It's been horrible, Aku. *Horrible!*' Avi's inherent penchant for the dramatic was in free flow. A stranger witnessing this side of Avi would possibly not be able to reconcile it with his grace under pressure just a few days ago. But then, Avi was a chameleon—always about the moment. And in this moment, his lament about the contest's sullied fate *demanded* drama, it seemed. 'Will this contest *ever* survive this scandal?'

'No doubt,' I told him drily. 'It will be topic of conversation for years to come. But rest assured, there will be a contest *every* year, regardless. This is *Eye India* we're talking about.

Why, even this year, despite all that has happened—we're *still* up for the finale. But Avi, I need you to listen. Tell me—do you by any chance happen to know a *Laddo* in this contest? It's a pet name I believe …'

'A *Laddo*?' Avi repeated, all attention now. We had that rapport, he understood nuance to the T. 'I don't think so.' I imagined him frowning in concentration at the name at the other end of the line. 'Why is this person so important to you, Aku?'

'Oh, just some message someone told me to give her, only I forgot to ask who *Laddo* was,' I said airily. My response was vague to the extreme, but Avi, wrapped up in narrating his anguish about the condition of the contest, didn't notice.

'Simply *awful,* this state of affairs,' he lamented. 'Enough to give us all nightmares.'

'I couldn't agree more,' I told him, shuddering. Avi didn't know just how much I sympathized with him on this point— my own nights had been full of foreboding. Restless, with that dark dream from a few nights ago still playing on my mind.

'Listen to me, Aku,' Avi whispered suddenly, lowering his voice. 'Y'know the night Lajjo died?'

'Yes,' I said, all ears now.

'I remember she had come to me before the rehearsal in the morning, saying she had a terrible stomach bug,' Avi confided. 'She said one of the mentors had offered to give her a natural remedy for it.'

'Go on,' I urged, realizing Avi was leading to something incredibly important.

'Aku—I know she was stabbed, so this has no real relevance,' Avi said. 'But somehow, I got a bad feeling about this when I remembered it yesterday. Do you think I need to notify the Addl.CP? Only we had so many mentors, and I didn't ask her which one ...'

'Avi, you need to tell Addl.CP Mhatre immediately,' my mind was racing as I conveyed this. We had so many mentors ... who on earth had offered to help Lajjo out that fatal day? And might it have anything to do with Parvati's poisoning theory?

'I've been going over it,' said Avi, sotto voce. 'The only logical conclusion would be Josy Joseph, because he's the health and fitness mentor ...'

I realized Avi was right. It was the second time Josy's name had come up as a possible suspect.

'You can't just accuse anyone, Avi,' I said cautiously. 'Just tell the police what you know. The rest is for them to figure out ...'

'I have spoken to the Addl.CP at length,' Avi continued. 'Several times in fact, though not about this. I only got back today, from all those *Eye India* meetings, anyway. Aku, there are some things the police are insisting on, about Lajjo, which baffle me, because they do not ring true.'

'Like what?' I asked Avi, concentrating so hard on him I almost dropped the phone in my eagerness to listen. I did not ask him about the meetings with his bosses that he mentioned. I knew that if he had wished to share something, he would have.

'They say Lajjo was under extreme stress. And was taking pills to help herself through it.' Avi said, then added, 'But Aku—Lajjo, over the many shows we've done together has *never* appeared stressed, no matter how high the tension. She just *wasn't* that person.'

I heard him out in silence. Once more, I believed Avi had said something of grave importance. Something that tied in to what we had learned earlier, when Parvati had quizzed the Addl.CP about a substance in Lajjo's system and he had mentioned that she was under terrific stress.

And here, once again, I couldn't agree more with Avi. Because the Lajjo I had known too was as cool as a cucumber. She wouldn't let anything ruffle her. Why, even when I had advanced from the front of stage in that final rehearsal, and Avi had announced for her to back off, she had done her part gracefully. Like a serene Madonna, no matter the rush of emotions churning within. So why were the police hellbent on calling her 'nervous'?

'Avi, I am with you on this one,' I told him, my voice grim. 'Lajjo just wasn't a skittish, nervy type. It is near-impossible she would be taking medication for a condition that she didn't have. So why do you think the police are insisting she was?'

'The Addl.CP said his team had asked two people connected to her and they both confirmed it,' Avi said. 'One was a doctor type, apparently.'

'Really?' I asked, still sceptical. 'Which doctor? Her private doc, or the hotel one?'

'I didn't ask the Addl.CP so much,' Avi said. 'I only know this bothered me.'

'It bothers me too,' I told him. 'It just doesn't sound like Lajjo ...'

I rang off, deeply troubled. So much had disturbed Avi, and he was acutely intuitive as a person. I often fed off this hyper-perceptive energy unconsciously, as people close to each other tend to do. In the past, it had only helped me. Today too, I saw no reason to doubt his sixth sense, and every reason to add my own misgivings to his. Lajjo's murder investigation had serious flaws. But how to help right them?

I dialled Jehaan, taking advantage of the fact that Roxanne hadn't returned from dinner yet.

'Aku,' Jehaan's voice sounded tight. He always sounded so around this time of the evening, it was approaching deadline for the next day's edition and he was heading the sports section after all. When it was like this, we were in perfect sync. We always spoke rapidly, and to-the-point, curtailing unnecessary dialogue so he could get back to work.

I filled him in on the day, as fast as I could manage. I stressed on sighting the mysterious stranger again, near the elevator, but being unable to get close enough to take a better look.. Then I told him about how I found the diary in another compartment of my bag, not the one I had put it in.

'You didn't leave your bag for a second?' Jehaan asked me.

'Not that I can recall,' I said. 'I had it with me when we met the Addl.CP, then ...'

But Jehaan was called away abruptly and apologizing, he hung up. He had already wished me luck for the finale, in case we didn't get to speak.

I tried to clear my head of everything that had transpired, and settled in to go to bed. Much as I wanted justice for all those so terribly and prematurely put to death, there was a contest I needed to ace, my raison d'etre for being here in the first place. And I wouldn't be able to do it without looking and feeling my best. So, a good night's sleep was essential. Everything else must wait, I decided.

The finale …

23

Akruti

～

'Are you going to sleep all morning?' a cheery voice said, in my ear, even as the curtain was pulled back, drowning me in soft, summery sunshine.

'It's D-Day!' Roxanne loomed over my sleepy face, brushing her hair vigorously. It appeared golden in the sun's rays, forming a halo round her face, she looked surreally angelic in that light. I smiled at her, trying to hold the moment before all the rest came tumbling into consciousness.

'What time is it?' I mumbled, looking over at my watch on the table.

'Time for you to get up and join me for breakfast!' Roxanne said. 'You didn't have any dinner last night, remember?'

'Yes, okay,' I acquiesced, giving in to Roxanne's well-meaning mothering. My stomach was growling anyway.

'We have the morning absolutely free!' Roxanne continued. 'By that of course it means that we can spend it being nervous and fidgety. So, let's at least have a nice breakfast. We're having it all together, downstairs!'

'Really?' I said my mind suddenly alert. No time like the now to ask everyone about *Laddu* once again! Maybe we'll be lucky?

We got ready and went down to the sunny, airy room we'd been assigned to eat in. It was, of course, separate from the other guests' areas.

Most of the girls were already present, sitting around a long table and chatting as they helped themselves to healthy food in miniscule portions. There was a charged atmosphere, at once electric and skittish—nervous energy before a big performance, now made raw by circumstance.

'Mood of the moment …?' Parvati said in my ear as she passed me to seat herself next to her roommate Tania.

I didn't reply. What was there to say?

'So what do you think, girls? Will this contest go smoothly?' Samantha asked, addressing nobody in particular. Her voice had been so loud though that conversation stopped and everyone tuned in.

'Why won't it?' Nina called out from the end of the table.

'Must I spell it out?' Samantha turned to her, slightly red in the face, her tone harsh, each syllable made more pronounced by anxiety.

'We've had a murder at *every* event for the past three nights,' Anuradha, Samantha's confidante, took up where she'd left off. 'Tonight is the biggest of them all. Do the math.'

There was a silence at Anuradha's vehement outburst. No doubt what she just voiced had been playing on all our minds, but to have it said openly like that was still a shock to the system.

'The police have a suspect. Tara's been taken in, remember?' Nina countered Anuradha gamely. 'Why should we panic now?'

'Come off it, Nina. Do you really believe Tara is a killer? That she murdered Lajjo or Doreen or Nuzhat?' Sanjna, the youngest among us had spoken up suddenly.

'Whether or not she believes it, the police do,' Tania rushed to Nina's defence. 'And they're the ones investigating this.'

'So, we're all happy about their verdict, is that it? Aishwarya, normally ultra-reserved, spoke up quietly. 'Do you honestly believe there is no danger now?'

There was silence at this, an uncomfortable silence, before Vandana spoke up, her face fearful. She had discovered Nuzhat with her head bashed in, along with Vanessa, and hadn't been quite herself post that. Unlike Vanessa, Parvati, Tania or I, who had undergone similar jolts, but had rallied—she couldn't absorb the intense shock.

'What do you mean?' she addressed Aishwarya, but the question was open to all.

'Vandana, let it be,' Vanessa said gently, because no one else would answer.

'Well, we know Tara couldn't really have killed Lajjo, don't we?' Pia spoke up hesitantly. 'So even if Tara did do something to Nuzhat without meaning to—she couldn't have stabbed Lajjo. We were all on ramp, she didn't do it. She was too far from her, right in the middle of ramp almost.'

'I know we shifted formation on ramp when we went to the restroom, and we've never discussed it among ourselves,' Smriti spoke up suddenly. 'But I want to tell you all, there hasn't been a time since that night that I've not gone over it in my mind, wondering if Nessie and I, we somehow *helped* Lajjo's killer … I'm so *so* sorry, girls …'

Tears glistened in Smriti's eyes, even as large-hearted Nisha rushed to comfort her.

'We couldn't help it,' Vanessa added. 'We *really* needed to use the restroom, we had no choice. It had been *such* a long day.'

'I don't see how you could have *helped* anyone stab Lajjo,' Nisha spoke plainly, one arm around Smriti. 'It's not like you took the knife and *stabbed* her.'

Collective cries at this vivid word picture that Nisha conjured up, and voices grew loud in protest.

'Stop it, Nisha,' Roxanne said severely, in her forthright manner. 'You don't have to go all graphic. Lajjo was one of us, remember?'

'I think Smriti means she feels she and Nessie helped the murderer *unintentionally*,' Inayat spoke up, her eyes troubled. 'Y'know there was a contestant among us, Doreen said …'

'Why do have to bring up Doreen now?' Myra wailed. 'Why are you all being so morbid? This is our last meal as equals. This evening someone will be crowned Miss India 1995, and we will no longer be like this. So why are we wasting this time scaring each other?'

'No one is scaring anyone, Myra,' Helen spoke up, her voice cultured and gentle. 'We are simply discussing something important, maybe what we ought to have discussed sometime ago—because it involves us all … especially as this is the finale night.'

'It might even help us somehow, now that we're finally *talking* about it,' Aishwarya said slowly. 'And no one is blaming you or Nessie, Smriti. You could not have known, could you …'

As the discussion intensified, Parvati met my eyes. Both of us were saying nothing. We wanted to see where it would lead, this unexpected parry, just a few hours to the big night. It was true, this was the first time post all that had happened that we were voicing openly what each of us felt.

The mood was nervous, speculative, but also suddenly, one of kinship. We were, all, after all, despite being competitors, in this together.

'If it wasn't Tara,' Pia said suddenly. 'Whose gown do you think could've concealed the knife that killed Lajjo? Remember, we all saw it later—it was *long*.'

Her words courted silence once more. We all knew in our hearts that Tara might not have been the one to stab Lajjo. Yet, we all hesitated at actually attempting to fill in the blanks with guesstimates. Maybe we were fearful of what we would actually uncover.

'Not longer than Myra's face ten days ago when we scared her so!' Anuradha suddenly spoke up, lightening the accumulated tension in a burst.

Some of the girls laughed. Not because they were being disrespectful to Lajjo, but because they were relieved by Anuradha's spontaneously light comment, allowing them to let go all the intensity of that built-up pressure. They didn't want to dwell on the frightening details of Lajjo's murder, clearly.

'What happened to Myra?' Sanjna wanted to know.

'Weren't you there that day?' Anuradha queried. 'We entered Myra's room as she was having her beauty sleep, all curtains and windows shut! She's such a scaredy cat, we wanted to play a prank. Samantha had covered her face with Myra's dupatta, that too. Can you imagine, Samantha leaned close to her ear and said 'I'm your alter ego' in a sinister voice! Sleep-dullened Myra, half-awake and sighting a shadow in her own dupatta, wouldn't stop screaming!'

As the girls chortled wickedly, I shivered slightly. The vividly described prank resembled my recent nightmare.

'But how did you get Myra's dupatta?' Sanjna asked, giggling but puzzled. 'We always lock our belongings, na?'

'You silly goose,' Anuradha said. 'We've been in this contest, living in this hotel for so long. Haven't you figured out by now that our keys work on each other's drawers? My drawer key fits my roomie's drawer. So must yours … how could you not know? Obviously, Myra's roomie, that's Samantha, got the dupatta out of her drawer using her own key, not Myra's!'

Giggling, Samantha added, 'We used the same technique to lock away part of Nina's costume in Nisha's drawer once! And they had connecting doors, Nina-Nisha and Lajjo-Pia, it was such fun we all laughed that day! You should've seen Nina's expression, her costume was an ode to her beloved SRK, and to have lost it, or have Nisha wear it, she couldn't decide which was worse!'

'Leave my SRK alone,' Nina's expression had lost its hilarity, she was dead serious even though the rest were laughing.

'Lajjo would've been more sporting,' Pia chided Nina softly, even as the rest curtailed their mirth.

Understanding and realization flashed simultaneously in Parvati's eyes. We realized why Pia was pushing to find Lajjo's killer at every opportunity today, however subtle. She had been her roomie and had obviously become fond of her.

More importantly, we realized how easily Parvati's diary, could've been taken. And going by the spate of revelations here … not just her roomie Tania—anyone of us, *anyone* of our keys … had access to her drawer.

24

From the pages of Parvati's diary

12 noon

Taking a breather. Some rather unexpected revelations at our last meal together as competitors and equals. It's noon now. In the lingering spirit of camaraderie, breakfast managed to stretch late into the morning. Quite an enlightening affair too. Sometimes, it takes just one flash for clarity … and then you can correct your course. One little revelation, that single missing piece—and voila! the entire puzzle is illuminated perfectly.

It happened to be like that today, when we all sat together, and so much became clearer. So much that we had kept to ourselves. Like Smriti's searing guilt at changing ramp formation the night Lajjo died. Or Vandana's anxiety, still haunting her, post discovering Nuzhat's body. Most importantly—the fact that not once among us truly believes Tara murdered anyone.

More revelations—as I had suspected, the keys, our drawer keys are all interchangeable. An oversight on the organizers' or the hotel's part, but with consequences that could be far-reaching. Who knows how things will turn out?

I tried once more to ask about *Laddo,* it was crucial to find this part of the puzzle. But it was also impossible to get the attention of everyone on this without drawing attention to why I wanted to know who she was.

The ones closest to me—Nina, Tania, Sanjna, Inayat—who heard my query, didn't bother to answer. The others were still laughing about various pranks. The mood had shifted by then, no one wanted to go back to the darkness. It would be the finale soon enough, and everyone was trying to make sure they were emotionally ready.

Even if the mood wasn't buoyant, given all that had happened, there was a sincere attempt to uplift it, ourselves. I wasn't allowed to play spoilsport. I had to leave it for the time being, however unwillingly.

1 p.m.

I know Akruti's mind is now almost entirely on the contest. There are only a few hours left to the finale. But I still made her sit with me, quietly, in a corner after our long, stretched-out meal, once the others left. We are so close to finding out who 'Laddo' is, but time is against us. We must do what we can, try our best despite the odds—how else to function? Pia's suggestion that we look to the gowns had got me thinking—why not continue along those lines?

We had actually explored that possibility yesterday, when Akruti and I were together. We had even reasoned as to which gown could be capable of concealing a knife, both of us convinced that its cut would need to be sleek. Before we could start listing the gowns on the girls however, the Addl.CP had sent for us and our attention had been diverted.

'All of us had long gowns,' Akruti said, a trifle impatient when I insisted on this brainstorming session before we got ready for the finale. 'It could've been anyone. Besides, we were thinking of this earlier, when the Addl.CP called us downstairs, and we didn't come up with any names, remember?'

'Because we were called downstairs,' I reminded her gently. 'Remember, a lot of us might have worn long gowns, but not all of us could stab like that. Stab with such force, stab so brutally that Lajjo really had no chance.'

Akruti stared at me. 'It would have to be someone who knew about weapons,' she said.

'Not necessarily,' I mused. 'Just someone who was quick and clever, deft at such work. Someone with strength, of course.'

'Like Josy, only, he wasn't up on ramp,' Akruti said, looking a trifle rueful that he wasn't, then added, 'It was a long blade. So for it to have been hidden, even partially, the gown would have had to be loose and flowing, not skin-tight.'

'Yes, you are right there,' I agreed. 'And it would have to be on one of the girls standing at the beginning of ramp, in the darkness, before midpoint. Because after midpoint, Lajjo was in spot, lit up. None of the girls from midpoint to ramp-edge touched her, as the camera showed, and when she reached you, she was already bleeding. So she had to have been stabbed earlier, as she walked ...'

'So whose gown was long and flowing, from all those standing up to midpoint?' Akruti said.

'After the formation change Roxanne stood midpoint. We all saw Lajjo pass her in spot as the music started. I doubt Pia, standing opposite Roxanne a little behind her, would've stabbed Lajjo—she was her roommate. If she wanted her dead she could've done it earlier. Besides, she was very close to midpoint too, the spot was on Lajjo by then, and Pia didn't move,' I asked.

'So that leaves Smriti and Vanessa, as usual. Nina, right at the back. Vandana, Tania, on one side of ramp, Nisha opposite them. And yes, Tara too,' Akruti met my eyes.

'Tara's gown was flowing, remember?' she said quietly.

'It might have been. But you don't believe that,' I retorted curtly. 'Tara isn't the one.'

'But we have to count her in,' Akruti's voice was steady. 'Smriti and Vanessa were in figure-hugging sheaths, rather difficult to manoeuvre a blade into, let's count them out.'

'Yes, they couldn't have done it.' I said, because I had followed them to their restroom break and back.

'That leaves Vandana, Tania, Nina, Nisha and of course, Tara ...' Akruti said.

'I don't see Tara as Lajjo's killer, call me stubborn,' I said. 'And Vandana is still in shock from having discovered Nuzhat—do you believe she would have the kind of temperament, quite frankly, the guts to stab anyone?'

'No,' Akruti said, doubtfully. 'You have a point, Parvati.'

'Which leaves us with Tania, Nina and Nisha,' I mused. 'This is getting murkier and murkier. So many suspects, no one a definite killer.'

'And all three girls had gowns on,' Akruti continued my guesswork. 'Flowy ones, capable of hiding a knife ...'

'We're forgetting something crucial,' I said to Akruti.

'Which is?' Akruti was losing patience and concentration, checking her watch as she spoke. The finale loomed, in a few hours, her mind was elsewhere.

'*The figure in the wings,*' I said.

'The one Addl.CP Mhatre asked us about?' Akruti asked, distracted. 'Yes ... *who was that?*'

'Too many players ... far too many. We're missing something,' I said, troubled, even as I scribbled all our deductions so far in the diary.

'Y'know, last night?' Akruti said, suddenly starting in recollection. 'You took the diary back to your room when

Roxanne came in. I was to call and tell you, but I had to talk to Avi. And I forgot about it after ... I'm sorry, Parvati.'

'It doesn't matter, Akruti,' I said gently. 'Remember what Samantha said earlier? *All* our keys fit all the drawers. So locking it up in your room wouldn't have helped either.'

'Sounds like you want it to be taken,' Akruti gazed at me speculatively, all her attention suddenly back on me.

I didn't answer her. But she wasn't that far from the truth. The finale would start soon. With barely any time left, I had come to a decision in the previous evening.

I *wanted* the person who had taken my diary to know we were onto them—how close we were now, to the truth. Akruti's revelation yesterday about the possibility of there being a third professional from the glamour world here, had opened up an avenue, a good lead. The missing puzzle pieces were slowly coming to light.

Maybe now, knowing we were getting closer to a breakthrough, they would lose their nerve, try something out in the open. With *me*. Dangerous, perhaps. But what part about this contest wasn't by now? And how else to narrow down the list of possible suspects? We were very nearly out of time, I needed to force this person's hand.

'So far, we know the killer is strong, *very* strong, almost an unnatural strength for a girl. Knows how to use a knife skilfully. Knows Doreen had information that might disqualify them, if they are a contestant. And that this person might be called *Laddo* ...' I said, writing all this down.

'And do you believe this person is a serial killer too?' Akruti asked, her eyes serious. 'That the *same* person killed *all three* of our colleagues? What I'm asking, Parvati, is—are we in danger again, at the finale tonight?'

I met Akruti's eyes with as much gravitas as I could muster without showing fear. I said nothing. What could I?

Finale night …

25

Akruti

Parvati was being typical Parvati—enigmatic, yet unfailingly logical—in that last meeting we had before we all disbursed to get ready for the big finale. She knew, as all of us did, that there might be more than a small element of danger present at the finale that evening. But she refused to voice her misgivings, even when I asked her point blank.

Honestly, I didn't have the time right then, to pursue what Parvati might know based on who she actually was, from what Jehaan had told me. My mind was almost entirely on the contest. I wanted to win, wanted it from deep within. The rest of it, mysterious, murky, terrifying—that could play itself out alongside.

I took her leave soon after, I needed to concentrate on the pageant at hand. I really couldn't do justice to that if Parvati kept urging me to brainstorm on the lengths and looks of gowns worn the night we lost poor Lajjo. The case would continue, I felt, but this night—it would only come once.

How do I describe the actual finale itself? How do I do justice to all that happened?

Let me start with the details. Some may call them inessentials, but every small detail contributes to the whole. My finale gown, for instance. I must tell you how I looked that night, it was a special gown for a special night. Gold and silver sequins enmeshed together, the silhouette figure-hugging, with an off-shoulder clingy bodice. The entire effect was almost mermaid-like.

This gown was what Avi had dreamed up for me when we had conversations centred on the crown ever since I had confided to him that I would be participating. He envisioned a gown of such radiance, that I was entranced. I strove to turn that into my reality, approaching all the masterful designers in the business. And that was what I finally ended up in, a gown with so much shimmer and shine, it drew all the lights on stage right to it ... and hopefully, to me!

Hair left loose and wild, to channel the sea-princess avatar some more. And shocking red lipstick, to complete the look. In a contest that had witnessed so much diversion, so much sorrow and so much horror—I needed to pull out all stops. Wow everyone on appearance alone, before getting to the brass tacks.

Preparation took a while. Everyone was to assemble in the green room constructed near the main outdoor stage for hair and make-up, around 5 pm. Earlier, if they could manage it. I took the liberty of doing my own make-up this time. And I needed the peace, alone, to make sure I looked my best. Face done, make-up bag in hand, I arrived at the welcome chaos of the green room sometime around 5.30 p.m.

The contest was scheduled to begin at 8 p.m. on the dot. Unlike at the earlier sub-contests, there would be no delays today. It was a made-for-television production, to be broadcast live nationally. No lapses or glitches would be entertained. If anyone had an attack of nerves and somehow couldn't be on stage—the show would go on without them. We had all been prepped, warned extensively about this. In fact we had been taught how to position ourselves so as to cover up absent spots in stage formation. This, so a watching audience wouldn't be able to tell if anyone was missing.

The judges had been instructed to be on time, there was a lot riding on flawless execution of this particular evening. Security was at a maximum—I caught a glimpse of Addl.CP Mhatre looking stern and imposing, as he instructed a posse of men in uniform and plainclothes a little distance away from the green room.

Inside the green room, the scene was familiar—the hum of hair equipment, the chatter of the contestants, the various members of the hair and make-up team. There were a dozen or so additional experts this time, because every girl had to look her best, and one make-up and hair artist wouldn't suffice.

'The diva arrives,' Roxanne announced, as I entered the room. No one really even bothered to look up. This was the moment of reckoning—I may have had the professional standing but today it was a fight to the finish. All of us had trained for this. Nothing was pre-written.

'You're looking lovely, Roxy,' I said, with a sudden rush of warmth for my roommate of almost three weeks, despite the tartness in her addressing me. She *was* too, all aglow, sheathed in baby pink. She scowled at me, then had the grace to blush.

My eyes searched for Parvati. I combed the sea of contestants as they preened in front of mirrors, or chatted in twos and threes. Glamorous and glittering as never before, all of them. Then, as Inayat and Anuradha parted ways in front of me, in striking red and blue respectively, they revealed Parvati's statuesque form. And I realized with a thrill how very magnificent she looked tonight.

Parvati's regal form appeared even more regal in the Audrey Hepburn updo of hair, complete with a miniature pearl tiara tucked cunningly in front. And the Grecian shell-white gown, flowy and figure-hugging in the right measure, held up on a shoulder with a single dazzling pearl-and-crystal brooch to complete the look. Gloves to match, ones that covered her arms up to the elbows. Unbelievable!

If I weren't so confident of my own appearance tonight, I would've been envious of hers. But as it went, I felt only a fierce joy, and to my surprise, an almost maternal pride for the girl in front of me. Her unlikely yet obvious transformation into this breath-taking vision had me floored. Whether or not Parvati was here to win this title, she certainly looked the part, I thought.

As I looked at her, a movement caught my eye. Beyond her, out the side entance of the green room, behind the gently wavering curtain. As it billowed high in a wayward gust of air, I saw him. The figure I had seen twice now, at the garden two days ago, and near the elevators more recently, that man conspicuous to me by his very attempt to appear inconspicuous. In a trice, I dashed past Parvati almost knocking her over to get to the green room side entrance.

But as usual, I was too late. When I reached the side entrance, having bumped into angry contestants along the way, the corridor outside was empty. Parvati reached me a split second later.

'What's gotten into you?' she asked quietly, using her hands to steady my panting frame. 'Why are you looking like you've seen a ghost?'

'He's *here*,' I hissed urgently. 'The guy from the elevator. The guy I had seen in the garden the other day. The one you think could be a reporter, only now I'm certain he's not. Reporters aren't allowed here!'

'There's no one outside right now,' Parvati's calm tone deflected my chagrin at losing him yet again. 'You need to concentrate *only* on yourself now.'

Parvati was right, of course. But my subconscious was still sending jangled messages. I sensed danger. Clear and very present once again, a red alert that wouldn't dissipate. 'There's a phone call for you, Parvati,' someone called out. 'They said it's important.'

Parvati turned and left me without saying another word. I watched her go, hoping it wasn't any disturbing family news at this crucial juncture. We could do without more bad news.

26

Akruti

'Akrrruti! Are you just about ready, my sweet? How do you look, sugar?!' Avi's familiar voice wafted over the din around me as I tried to silence my instinct for the moment and clear my head of the dark cloud that threatened to envelop it. I looked up to see him pushing past the contestants in front of me.

'Well, aren't we a vision?' He nodded approvingly, after casting a critical eye on my make-up and outfit. My hair wasn't done still, but this was Avi, he knew how to envision what *would* be, from what *was* in front of him. And he and I, we had our particular rhythm anyway, he knew how I would look once the war paint was completely on.

'I'm glad to see you Avi,' I told him, suddenly realising how utterly and completely true that was. I needed his moral support, my instinct was warning me to be on my guard but I had no idea against what.

'Akruti, you need to focus on the crown now,' Avi said, matter of fact, but his eyes were saying other things.

'What is it? Tell me?' I asked fiercely.

'The Addl.CP will speak to you,' Avi held me close, and whispered in my ear. 'The blade that killed Lajjo? *Your fingerprints were on the handle.*'

190

'But how?' I whispered, drawing back as if slapped, struck dumb for a second. 'I never touched it.'

'Neither did you stab her on stage. There were enough witnesses who saw her collapse and you hold her. But regardless—the handle on the blade shows *only* your prints ...'

'Will he arrest me now?' I asked, suddenly wary. 'And why wait so long if they found my prints on the blade? It's been three days ...'

'I think they were trying to find out *when* you could've possibly done it. You were in full view of everybody that entire rehearsal. You even sat in front of ramp, actually entered from there. It's most baffling,' Avi went on. 'He said this to me in confidence, hoping I could shed some light on it. This morning in fact, but I've been in two minds whether to tell you. The contest is so important to you. Also, I believe he suspects foul play. So he's hesitating to arrest you. Given your high profile, it wouldn't do to have to backtrack if he's made a mistake.'

'I see,' I said. 'Glad your loyalty to me won out, Avi,' I added, grateful that he'd chosen to tell me.

'Always, Aku,' Avi said. 'But do you know how *your* fingerprints could have got onto the weapon's handle?'

'No idea,' I told him, genuinely at a loss.

My mind was whirling, no wonder my instinct was warning me of danger. Getting arrested before the contest was no laughing matter. I hadn't killed Lajjo, but just going through all the motions to prove it would sap me of much. I had no wish to be in that position at all, especially not now.

'All I remember touching were the tap-dancing sticks for the opening routine,' I told Avi. 'The pre-contest dance for television, the one where all the contestants are introduced on stage. They cancelled it after what happened, now it's a more sombre show given what we've been through. But while we were practising, everyone had a stick and a tall hat. But there were no blades, none.'

'Are you sure, Aku?' Avi asked.

I was. My memory was unwavering on this. I may not have noticed crucial lapses during that fatal rehearsal where Lajjo was stabbed. Or the exact conversation while I talked to Doreen, but my memory was exacting when it concerned any strenuous effort towards the crown. I hadn't handled a blade, not ever.

'Is the Addl.CP going to dramatically walk in and take me into custody anytime soon, Avi?' I asked, extremely wary now. My big dream, that singular shot at the Miss India crown— It was never in more danger of utter collapse than at this moment, with Avi's devastating news of an impending arrest.

'Let's hope not,' Avi muttered darkly. 'But *Eye India* will really have a lot to say there, I think ...'

What Avi was conveying was that at least till the finale was done, there was time. *Eye India*'s influence may have bought it for me, but I was not complaining. I intended to use every bit of it.

'Why don't you get your hair done?' Avi said, matter of fact as ever. 'You've been given this much, you're here still. The contest isn't over.'

'No it's not,' I said, chin up now, as I checked the time. It was almost 6.30 pm, an hour since I got here. 'I'm going to do just that, Avi.'

Deeply disturbed and on edge, I moved towards the area in the green room where the girls were having their hair done. I was lost in thought as the hairdresser blow-dried and curled my tresses to perfection. My look channelled a wild-child mermaid, but I was feeling more like a little girl lost.

Alone with my thoughts, I was tapped on the shoulder by someone as I got up from the hair-dressing chair. I looked up, distracted from all that was on my mind. And looked into the eyes of Gokul—Doreen's hairdresser husband.

Shock hit me like electricity, and I would've stumbled but for his steadying hand. I met his glistening eyes and felt my own grow teary. I took both his hands in mine.

'I'm so sorry, Gokul,' I told him. 'It shouldn't have been this way. She was so full of life.'

'Yes,' Gokul was finding it hard to speak through his emotion. 'I came as fast as I could. Then the police wanted me to speak with them. They've been questioning me ...'

My heart ached for this poor simple soul, bereft of his voluble, effervescent companion forever. He looked both lost and despairing, like he didn't have a clue where he was and how he'd gotten here.

'I just wanted to wish you luck,' he said simply, through his tears. 'Doreen knew you were my favourite, she would've liked that I met you to tell you that. I wasn't supposed to be here for this assignment. But fate's ways ...'

'Thank you, Gokul,' I said gently. 'Doreen told me you were rooting for me. I was glad.'

Suddenly like a light had been switched on, the rest of my conversation with Doreen came back to me in a flash. And despite the inappropriateness of the timing, I knew what I had to do.

'Gokul,' I watched him, intently. 'Gokul, I need to know something ...'

'About Doreen?' he asked listlessly. 'I've told the police all I know ... I have no clue who would want to do this to her. And so heartlessly, so wickedly ...'

I kept silent, trying to think of a delicate way to approach this. How would Parvati do it?

Also, something was disturbing me, something I couldn't quite put my finger on. Something I knew was very important.

I tried to focus on the task at hand. And it came to me, how Parvati would do it. Also, how I must use the same approach. So I got right to it.

'Gokul,' I said, 'Who is *Laddo?*' I asked the question artlessly, without guile, straight out, like Parvati would. Something about my query disturbed me, not the question itself ... my uneasiness had something to do with Parvati. Why this awful feeling?

Gokul opened his mouth to speak, but in that instant there was a loud crash. A crash that shook the makeshift green room to its foundation, such that the lights went out. In the shrieking that followed, absolute pandemonium, as contestants ran helter-skelter, screaming.

Lights going out was no cause to panic but this contest had us all on edge from Lajjo's stabbing, four nights ago. We were conscious that a serial killer might be on the loose, it was uppermost on our minds that entire day since our collective discussion at lunch. And the sudden darkness in the green room brought on abject hysteria.

I found myself running alongside everybody else in the darkness, as agitated, as utterly panicked as I'd ever been. But unlike the rest, I knew where I was headed. Gokul had uttered a single name and despite the resounding crash, I had caught it. Suddenly, awfully, I was in my nightmare again, the one in which the veiled hant was clutching at me, crown in hand. Relentless with cold, dead fingers, even as I ran, even as I tried to escape. *Parvati ...*

27

Akruti

The corridor seemed endless. Bleak darkness surrounded me as I stumbled on. The terror wouldn't let go, everything seemed a blur. Because in the green room, even as Gokul had revealed the name we had been trying so hard to figure out all this while, it hit me—*Parvati was missing*.

She had been summoned to attend to an urgent call almost two hours ago. And she hadn't returned. Caught up in my own situation—Avi's cautionary news and then Gokul's arrival—I had not kept track of the time lapse, realising her absence only when the feeling that something was very wrong became overpowering.

Her absence wouldn't have been a big deal, but for the fact that this was finale night. Knowing Parvati's upright nature and how she was a stickler for rules, she wouldn't have tried to veer off-path on finale night. Besides, my instinct was buzzing so much it was like a siren clanging, a warning that nothing was right at present.

As I ran, the name Gokul had uttered played over in my mind. How could we not have realised it earlier? Parvati had even written the clues down in her precious diary. *A person with strength, almost unnatural strength,* she had written. I knew now—we had witnessed this manner of strength, all of us had, at one of the pre-contests.

A person who knows how to handle a knife. Of course, this person was in training for exactly this. And such deception! We'd all been fooled.

At last, out-of-breath, I reached my destination. The two minute distance from the open air stage and adjacent green room to here had taken a while because everything was pitch-black.

Cautiously, I felt my way inside. Why was I here? Because I knew, as everyone did, that the lone phone for urgent calls was placed here for our convenience. If Parvati had indeed been summoned for a phone call, this is where she'd have come.

As I shuffled cautiously inside the lightless room, I heard a click. The beam of a powerful torch cast a singular but insistent glow through the narrow room, revealing two figures. They stood directly ahead, facing each other. I peered at them anxiously. One of them, to my relief, was Parvati!

She stood in front of me, framed in the light the torch cast, the frontal glare partially blinding me to the other person's face, save for a dark silhouette.

'Parvati,' I said, urgency making my sentences come out all breathless. 'What took you so long? You've been gone two hours. The contest starts bang on time, and it is 7.45 p.m. now. Whose phone call was it? Is everything okay?'

'Shhhh,' Parvati said. She wasn't looking at me, but straight ahead at the person standing in front of us both, still in darkness because of the blinding glare of the torch.

I shifted my position, edging closer to the silhouette to see who it was. To my horror, I realized the person wasn't just holding the torch, but a knife too. The blade glistened in the half-light.

'Hello Akruti. So nice of you to join us,' Nina said.

'Nina,' I said, more shocked than afraid. 'What are you doing?'

'I think you should call me by my pet name, since you seem to be familiar with it, anyway,' Nina said, putting the torch on the table nearby so that it's glare lit all three of us. Both her hands now clutched the knife. Her eyes glittered, as if with ferocious purpose. "You two have finally found me,' she said.

'Meet *Laddo*,' Parvati said quietly, without irony. With a start I realised I was indeed, finally, facing the elusive Laddo; the name Gokul had whispered to me just a while back. In the relief of finding Parvati safe, I had overlooked that for a nanosecond, but the situation now demanded absolute attention.

'Not to be confused with Lajjo, ofcourse, though there were times I wished it could be,' Nina was saying. 'How much I wished I could be such a natural forerunner, winning so many pre-contests, just as she was doing.'

Parvati gestured to me to keep my silence and expression neutral but I couldn't help gawking at Nina.

'What's the big deal?' Nina's eyes shone with a decidedly manic light as I watched her, flabbergasted. 'Just remove the 'j' for 'joy'. And add 'd', like in 'death', double the dose, of course … and Lajjo becomes *Laddo* …'

'*Why*?' I asked Nina, confounded by both her explanation and ambition. '*Why* would you want to become Lajjo, Nina?'

'Because I couldn't become YOU!' Nina faced me, her expression suddenly bitter. 'Miss Snow White, straight out of the beauty magazines, as if made for the fairy-tale crown. Radiant, aren't you, with your cat eyes and bleached skin-tone? The nation's darling. *Such a strong contender for the title,* said the media in all the reports. No, no one could become *you.'*

'But Lajjo,' Nina continued rapidly, 'her dark skin, her dark eyes—her beauty is *accessible,* we *all* have it in some measure. If we tried hard, if people like Avi noticed, with luck and timing and effort … we could all be Lajjo. She was your *only* real competition. She rewrote the rules, y'know. Made it okay for people with dusky features, *normal* features, to still be in the running for this crown. She, NOT YOU!'

'So you'd rather *be* her?' I said, still not understanding, ignoring Parvati's frantic efforts to make me keep my silence.

'How else could I have the crown, if I couldn't be you? The chances of her winning were almost equal to yours, she was a very strong dark horse, if I can say that,' she cackled at her own joke, then eyed me cunningly, 'I killed Lajjo, so I could take her place as a strong contender. And even better if you were labelled her murderer, don't you agree? Then the way to the crown is absolutely anyone's game. So why not mine?'

'Nina, *what are you saying*?' I asked, filled with cold dread. I hadn't been afraid when she had pointed the knife at us, nor at the odd look on her face. But as she began to talk of Lajjo, I suddenly woke to the fact that Parvati and I, we were now part of a very dangerous scenario. Nina, or as we now knew, *Laddo*, was actually *confessing* to murder.

'It would be so easy, wouldn't it? All the Addl.CP needs to do is arrest you,' Nina was muttering, almost to herself. 'Why is he dragging his feet over it? Your prints are on the blade that killed her …'

'How would you know that, Nina?' I asked, my every sense on high-alert. I knew I needed to keep her talking.

'Don't aggravate her,' Parvati whispered to me, the warning note in her voice sharp. 'Leave her be.'

How Nina had deceived us all, pretending to be shy and weak, fainting at Lajjo's death, crying out, wide-eyed in fear as the Addl.CP told us we were all suspects the night Lajjo was stabbed. How dramatic her shock when Tara was accused, how innocent her expression at Parvati's repeated queries about *Laddo*. And here she was now, cool as a cucumber, discussing Lajjo's murder with such cold blooded precision.

'Then all I had to do was ensure that I won, *and I would* … and soon, soon—Bollywood!' Nina was still muttering, her eyes feverishly aglow. 'I would get to be with my SRK, that's Saurav Roop Kamal to you. Star with him in a movie, not as a sidey in the background, but as a lead actor, as a Miss India winner. He wouldn't dare ignore me then, he would *know* me. *Know who I am!*'

Parvati was edging close to Nina as the girl spoke, taking advantage of the fact that Nina's attention was fixed on me. Now, in a sudden swoop, she lunged forward, knocking the knife out of Nina's hands, and picking it up herself in one smooth movement.

But she hadn't accounted for the fact that Nina was surprisingly strong. We had seen this earlier, at the talent round, when the seemingly timid Nina had leaped astonishingly-swiftly to save the chair prop from tumbling off-stage into the audience. Her powerful arms had guided the half fallen missile safely back up, and we had all marvelled at her quick reflexes.

'Watch out, Parvati,' I screamed, as Nina moved, lightning quick. She used her wiry, muscular frame to twist round slender Parvati, who instantly buckled under the strain. A tussle broke out for the knife, Parvati's slim form versus Nina's muscular silhouette.

I leaped forward to help Parvati best I could, but I was out of luck. The torch, all this while throwing eerie shadows of the struggle on the wall opposite, was knocked off the table with a crash. For a second or so, the room was pitch-dark and utterly silent.

Just for a heartbeat, that unnerving quiet pervaded, moment enough for each of us to assess the situation. Then a voice spoke up. Calm, without a trace of hysteria, echoing in the stillness: 'Parvati, you would do well to leave *Laddo* alone.'

The torch was picked up, switched back on and aimed at us. I caught Parvati's grim face before I felt the sting of a knife at my throat, before I smelled an all too-familiar perfume, before I even registered the voice which had just spoken—*a voice I knew very well, indeed.*

28

Akruti

'Drop the knife, Parvati! It will not help you now,' Lubaina Pervez's strong, well-enunciated voice spoke commandingly in my ear as she addressed Parvati. She was holding another knife to my throat. Her heavy perfume, at such close quarters, made me nauseous in that narrow, airless room. As contestants, all of us had known that smell—it had signalled Lubaina's arrival.

'We could go on playing this cat-and-mouse game, but you know I have the ace now,' she went on. 'Or shall I say the queen? Queen Akruti, hot contender for the crown.' She laughed softly near my ear.

Infront of me Parvati, stony-faced, had allowed Nina to take the knife back. She stood facing us now, still.

Lubaina let the knife slide off my throat and moved next to me, so that two of us were now facing two of them. She had nicked me a bit with the knife, enough to draw some blood, but it was unimportant right then. I allowed myself to breathe.

Watching Parvati struggle with Nina had felt like a punch in the gut, and now *this*. I wasn't sure what I felt at that moment. Terror? Despair? Incredulity? A mix of all three summed it up, maybe.

'Smart girl,' Lubaina said, as Nina brandished the knife, pointing it at Parvati once more, her eyes glittering dangerously. A bruise, purple and angry was already forming over Parvati's right temple.

'Part of having a superior intelligence is knowing when to step back. And you are no fool, Parvati, I'll give you that,' Lubaina said. She had her knife pointed at me, but her tone seemed casual, like the one she used in class while mentoring us. We could've been at one of her sessions for all the matter-of-factness in her manner. There was no threat in her tone, simply knowledge. But oddly, that made it even more menacing to me.

'So here we are,' Lubaina said. The torch she had picked up during the tussle was back on the table, illuminating us in a shadowy half-light.

'A little diversion from this situation,' Lubaina was saying, as if she was talking about the weather. 'They've managed to get the lights out on the stage to start working, though much of this area here is still in darkness. The contest has begun, you can hear the music. Sadly—both of you won't be participating.'

The first part of her speech was true enough, I realised with a start. I had been concentrating so hard on what was going on inside this room, that I had blocked out everything else. Now it all came pouring into my consciousness—the music, the beginning strains of the opening number, the compere introducing the judges. The contest was in progress. Despite the inherent terror, a blinding rage gripped me. I was supposed to be out there. I was supposed to be on stage. How had they begun without noticing that contestants were missing?

And then, dully, the voice of reason in my head provided the answer to that query—it was a made-for-television event;

of course they would begin, regardless of last-minute lapses. We had been cautioned earlier that it would indeed be so. The show would go on, with or without me.

'Yes, it must hurt,' Lubaina was watching me, as she spoke again, this time with great malice. 'To know that your dearest dream is taking place at this very moment *without* you in it. It must be awful. You must be in pain ...'

Then her voice turned deep, hard; as if rocked with unfathomable emotion.

'But it's nothing compared to the pain I've been through,' she said much too loudly. 'The pain, the awful pain of the loss of the one dream you held closest to your heart. A living, breathing dream, one you nurtured and believed in and encouraged for years and years. Till a cruel twist of fate took it away. Took *her* away—the one without whom life is meaningless ...'

Parvati's incomprehensible expression changed, her face showed some understanding. 'Lubaina ...?' she said, her voice oddly hesitant.

'Do you know what it's like?' Lubaina continued, almost as if speaking to herself. She seemed to have forgotten we were in the room with her.

'Can you even understand? I doubt your pea-size skulls could fathom the magnitude of such loss.' Her voice rose and fell as she spoke. '*Real* loss, not candy floss sashes and crowns. To have a bright, beautiful dream given to you after years and years of trying to conceive. To be fortunate enough to receive such a gift, to watch it bud and grow, as you lovingly tend it, day after day, year upon year ...'

Parvati watched Lubaina, listening intently. I watched Parvati. We both ignored Nina, who seemed to have shrunk somehow, in front of Lubaina's towering personality and her all-consuming grief.

'My brave, beautiful child. She was so beautiful. Year upon year as I came to work here, as I mentored every new hopeful, I thought, "One day it will be my baby here." And then two years ago, it was.'

Lubaina seemed to stiffen at the memory. Then she continued. 'Only my child, my precious sweetheart—she wanted to look perfect. I told her it was nothing, there was no need for cosmetic surgery, for such a little thing, such a *very* little thing ... But she insisted, and I relented. This is the twentieth century, so many people have had cosmetic surgeries safely, so why not her? And they botched it up.'

Lubaina's perfectly modulated voice dropped here, guttural, strangulated. Then it rose, a yowl of pure pain, inhuman. '*They botched it up*. My angel, my sure-shot beauty queen, my perfect child. My Shilpi. She *died*.'

Lubaina's voice cracked and broke, fading abruptly. In the resulting silence, the music outside didn't register. Parvati and I were rooted to our spots, shell-shocked at this revelation of terrible tragedy. Only Nina seemed to not understand the poignancy of the moment. She shifted impatiently, one foot to the next, her gimlet eyes darting towards me and Parvati by turn, glittering in the torch light.

'Which one first?' she murmured, the whites of her eyes showing, her voice unnatural to our ears. 'Tell me, aunt L!'

'Shilpi, stop talking.' At being addressed by Nina, Lubaina seemed to have come out of her emotional trance. 'Hush, my child ...'

But it was Parvati who couldn't keep silent now. '*Aunt L*? It falls into place now. She's your *niece*, isn't she? Nina, aka *Laddo*?' she addressed Lubaina. 'That's why she had to bend the rules to be here. She wouldn't be allowed, she's related to a mentor.'

'Yes, that's right,' Nina spoke up now, leering at Parvati. 'I *am* her niece. And I had to participate, how else would I be taken seriously in the glamour business? Life's tough for small-town girls like me. I needed to star in a film with SRK— this was the easiest, shortest way to gain access to Bollywood without a Godfather, you must know this. And so I bent the rules. Why not? Such silly rules too.'

But Lubaina wasn't in the mood for Nina's self-indulgent chatter. 'Hush I said, Shilpi. I need to think.'

Something struck me as odd, before I could think it out, I was voicing it. 'Why does she keep calling you Shilpi?' I asked Nina.

'Shilpi was my cousin,' Nina turned towards me, sharp dislike in her eyes, but she answered, even then. 'Aunt L's only child, used to model long ago. She died. Cosmetic surgery gone wrong. I look like her, many people in the family think it's uncanny how much. My aunt forgets sometimes ...'

Looking at aunt and niece standing near each other in the dim torchlight, I realized with a start why Lubaina's face had seemed so familiar to me in early training sessions. It wasn't because she might have modelled in her youth as I had then supposed ...

It was because her daughter Shilpi had been a model, and I had caught the resemblance between them. Before my time, and yet, it was remarkable that I had caught that, only couldn't quite place how. It was startling how Nina too had it, up close and personal.

Parvati met my eyes. Lubaina didn't seem 'forgetful' as Nina said—she seemed unhinged. In fact, both members in this family appeared dangerously deranged, albeit in different ways. Their varying levels of obsessiveness were starkly obvious now. *How had we not noticed earlier?* Not their obsessiveness, nor their resemblance to each other. We were conscious of the unsaid, as we looked at each other—how were we to resolve this terrible dragnet without further loss of lives?

29

Akruti

⌒

'Why won't you answer me, Aunt L?' Nina repeated. 'Tell me which one to kill first …'

'To *kill*?' Parvati said, her voice impassive. 'Surely you are confused, Nina? You don't mean that.'

I watched Parvati, she was upto something. Nina wasn't confused, no one could doubt the intent in her voice. Or the menace.

'No, Shilpi isn't confused,' Lubaina seemed to have registered Parvati's question and hastened to correct her. 'You both need to be dealt with. *How else will my beautiful girl win the crown?*'

'The original plan was to only kill Lajjo,' Nina broke in, addressing Parvati. 'You were never a threat in the contest.'

'So why now?' I asked, following Parvati's lead, hoping to find answers even in this grim situation.

'Because she found out too much. She was so close to figuring it all out, our game plan. We couldn't risk her knowing more. We saw her diary, you know. On three occasions. But also—she asked for me by my pet name. Twice, in fact— once announcing that *Luddo* had a phone call, I saw right through that. And the second time at our breakfast together, those present ignored her question. But sooner or later, she would've found out,' Nina said.

'You stabbed Lajjo? On ramp?' Parvati, ever-direct, asked Nina.

'Yes, it was easy,' Nina smirked. 'Lajjo was to die on stage, stabbed so artfully, like in some movie with SRK. Romantic and tragic. *And she did.*'

'You know, they really do teach medicine very well, in my home-town,' she continued. 'I might be Miss India, but I am a med student too. I knew exactly where to drive the blade in. She might not have felt much pain in her drugged state, but the damage was extensive and fatal because that stab wound would draw maximum blood.

Aunt L handed me the blade from the wings in the black-out, even waited till I actually stabbed her. I was last in the line-up, standing just in front of Lajjo. I stabbed her when she passed me in the darkness. The music hadn't even begun, she pre-empted it, in her witless state. The spot wasn't on either, and the girls were shifting formation in front of me, so there was a bit shuffling in the darkness. It was too easy in the chaos.

Aunt L had drugged her earlier, with the colourless, odourless psychotropic drug I'd given her, again courtesy my medical training. Lajjo had been unwell that morning, Aunt L insisted she have some water before she went onstage. Told her it had a natural remedy mixed in it, to help her feel better. It took fifteen minutes or so for the drug to take effect. Timed perfectly to happen just at blackout, in fact, she would've been perfectly normal before that. Of course, Avi's music change was a little off-putting, because Lajjo moved before she had to, she was confused. We managed, despite that hiccup. Lajjo may have felt the knife, I don't know. But she was so drugged, she didn't even scream. Of course she did stumble a little later on ramp, when the effects of the drug and the blood loss both took hold.'

'How horrible,' I murmured under my breath, thinking of the whole awful scenario, now laid before me so plainly.

'Oh, it wasn't horrible at all,' Nina has caught my words. 'It was delightful. Knowing as the blade went in, that she would not be in the contest anymore. Knowing that this would be her last walk.'

Nina's smiling face changed abruptly. Looking suddenly annoyed, she turned to face me. 'It's too bad you weren't where you were supposed to be, Akruti,' she said. 'You spoiled it a bit, by entering impromptu from the front of stage instead of the wings like you always did.

The plan was to have you implicated in the stabbing when you walked from behind her to take your place. But so much went awry. The music changed suddenly, throwing off our timing. The girls went off-stage and shifted formation, there was such chaos on ramp. I had to be really clever to stab her so quick without bumping into anyone or being noticed. And then, you—you walked from the front, so you were nowhere near Lajjo when she was stabbed. You caught her as she fell, but unfortunately, it was in full public view. Bit awkward, that, when the blade handle showed your fingerprints …

Y'know that was ingenuous actually. The blade slips into the tap dance stick, fits snugly inside, no one would notice if they didn't know—all of it goes in, save the handle. So when we practised for the opening dance, Akruti was holding the stick with the blade sheathed within. When we removed it from the disguise of the stick—her fingerprints were on it! Aunt L's idea, that!'

I shuddered, thinking I had actually held the blade that went through Lajjo without knowing it. And now I could finally place where it was that I had seen that intricately carved handle on the blade itself—it was part of tap-dancing sticks I'd trained with. I had recalled having seen that design somewhere when I first saw the weapon driven clean through Lajjo's back, but in shock had forgotten about my effort at partial recognition till now.

'That's how dear Aunt L got the blade into the wings as well,' Nina was explaining. 'Till the last moment everyone thought she was carrying one of the dance sticks. And she was a mentor, no one would stop her being in the wings at the rehearsal of the finale.'

Parvati met my eyes. We now knew who the shadowy figure on the recording Mhatre had shown us was. Lubaina, allowed there as a mentor, watching her niece *Laddo* drive the blade into Lajjo in the semi-darkness of blackout. No gown had concealed the murder weapon. It had been carried right through to the stage wings by a trusted mentor, then handed to her deranged niece in full view of everyone present, should they have cared to pay attention. Yet no one had noticed the exchange at all, courtesy the darkness.

'Poor, poor Lajjo,' the words escaped me involuntarily.

'Yes,' Nina said, cool and unruffled, save for the odd gleam in her eyes. 'Poor Lajjo. She went first. Then Doreen. And finally Nuzhat.'

'Why Nuzhat? She was not a forerunner in this pageant. So why kill her?' Parvati asked quietly.

'To distract the police. To pin the blame of *all* the murders on Tara who had an ill history with Nuzhat especially. To divert attention from us completely. Tara is so nervous, she makes an easy suspect for a serial killer and she had scuffled with Nuzhat as well, earlier,' Nina replied, leering at Parvati once more. 'We *had* to divert attention from us. Especially as you were looking for me. For *Laddo* as you said in your diary ... well, you found me. And it could only be this way. I had to get rid of you, I was the one who called out in the green room that you had an urgent phone call. I lured you out, then followed you here to the telephone room. It's too bad the lights went out just as you got here. Such a pain running back to my room, locating that camping torch, then running back down again. I knew you might stay put here, there were no lights, you would wait till they came on. And you did.'

'Yes,' Parvati's face showed no emotion. 'I waited.'

'I wish Doreen had waited,' Nina told her suddenly. 'She was such a chatterbox. There was no need for her to die. But she wouldn't stop talking about my bending the rules to be here. She knew Aunt L was related to me. Gokul had told her. He had come to my hometown, long ago, once. He had done my make-up for a small role in SRK's film then. I was performing a background dance, SRK didn't even look at me first. But one day, I slipped doing my steps near him and he helped me up. Such a wonderful smile. *And I knew.* I knew I would follow him here and act with him, and he would notice me as he never did then.'

Nina paused for breath. Talking about SRK had always gotten her worked up, but we never realised how bad it was, her obsession.

'I had confided in Gokul, I told him I would be a Bollywood heroine to get to SRK. He said I could start modelling, then try my luck at Miss India. I told him Aunt L was my aunt, I never knew the rules then, that I had to keep it a secret. Even later, Gokul promised he'd never tell. Only his wife, she already knew, he had told her. If only she had kept quiet. But she went on and on and on …'

Once more, Nina turned to me. 'It was lucky I was there when she began telling *you*,' she said. 'I was seated behind the dressing cubicle curtain. But you didn't ask more and the topic changed. Good for you.' Here she smiled crazily. 'Else I'd have had to kill you earlier than this.'

'You went back to kill Doreen?' Parvati spoke up. 'From the swimsuit round?'

'I never left the green room,' Nina said to her. 'I was waiting behind the curtain all the while that Inayat was getting ready, and Doreen was blabbing freely. She even told Inayat my name, but it was drowned by the music being tested on stage, and that dimwit Inayat never heard. Or realized how close she'd come to being murdered as well. Then the other two girls finished their hair touch-ups and left. I was alone with Doreen. I seized the moment. I used her own scissors to kill her. You should've seen Doreen's face at the end, pleading for her life. Of course, I had to wipe the scissors clean, after. Wouldn't do to have my prints on the weapon, would it? Especially since we made sure that Queen Akruti's prints were on the blade handle that killed Lajjo!'

I don't know how Parvati's expression could remain so impassive, I was overcome with disgust, rage and repulsion all at once at the extent of depravity in this girl's confession. But I kept quiet. Agitating her would not do.

'You were present when Tara and Nuzhat scuffled?' I asked, just to get away from the graphic image in my mind of Doreen's final moments.

'Yes, I was in the restroom nearby. Tara hit Nuzhat in sheer desperation, because Nuzhat was maliciously teasing her. Nuzhat was dazed, after the blow, but still conscious. Tara left for her stage appearance. That's when it came to me immediately, how I could turn Nuzhat's misfortune into my opportunity. So I walked up and finished the job. No one saw me. I bashed in Nuzhat's head, and made sure Tara was implicated later, by whispering to Tania about the scuffle infront of the Addl.CP. Many others had heard it as well. The rest was easy. The police went after Tara. *And now no one will know about our role in the killings.'*

'No one, that is, except for you two,' Lubaina, utterly silent and in her own world all this while, suddenly spoke up. 'Shilpi, you cannot kill one first, then the other—there's no time. You have to be on stage very soon, they will be announcing the finalists in a few moments, based on points and judging of the pre-contests.'

My heart sank at this. I knew very soon they would start calling out the names of those who would be part of the final round—the all-powerful Q&A round.

'Shall we knife them together?' Nina asked her aunt, looking positively sickly in her pleasure at saying this.

'No, we'll lock them in, torch the room,' Lubaina said decisively, in her perfectly-modulated voice. It occurred to me just how twisted the minds of the two of them, both aunt and niece, were. Frighteningly so.

'How did you read my diary?' Parvati suddenly asked loudly. At her words, I realized the utter despair in our predicament, over and above my rage and disgust with this duo. I knew she was trying to buy time. But even with extra time, how were we to get ourselves away from these two?

'Tania, your roommate, took it out of your drawer the first time,' Nina said. The organisers rely too much on contestants being upright and honest—how silly to give keys that will fit every drawer! What is private then? Anyway, I convinced Tania to get it for me. I read it, *all of it,* especially the 'need to find *Laddo*' part.

The thing is, my sweet Parvati, no one here would know about the name *Laddo.* Gokul knew it because he had helped me earlier in my hometown, and because he used it, so too did Doreen. But luckily for me, her loose tongue didn't spill the beans on my pet name. I silenced her before it could do more harm to me.

Anyway, Tania hates to read, and she didn't bother reading your diary, though she's curious by nature. She left it to me, assuming that we were making a note of your secrets. She didn't know the manner of those secrets … That's why I could get her to do it again, last night as well.'

'I removed it from Akruti's bag the second time,' Lubaina drawled. 'While you both were busy doing Josy Joseph's meditation in the corridor when we met you. You had given it to her for safekeeping but I was smarter, looked through both your bags after offering to hold them for you.'

'*That's why* the diary was in a different compartment in my bag from where I'd put it,' I spoke up. 'I *knew* I hadn't made a mistake, I was puzzled as to how it got to another pocket. But I never thought of you.'

'You should have,' Lubaina told me, coolly. 'It would've spared you all of this. It was only supposed to be Lajjo. I even told the Addl.CP how Lajjo was a nervous creature, used to taking meds to calm herself. This, in case the post-mortem discovered the drug in her system.'

'And I roomed right next to her. I made all possible use of my med training. I told the police the same thing, even stating I had the medical credentials,' Nina added.

'No wonder they were convinced Lajjo was an anxious person,' I said. 'It just wasn't true, and you two made sure they were convinced otherwise.'

'A respected mentor responsible for contestants' well-being, and a medically trained "best friend" on call nearby if necessary, who ascertained Lajjo was a 'nervous' sort. Why would the police suspect foul play?' Lubaina asked, a thin half-smile playing on her lips. This chilled us even more than Nina's cold eyes—Lubaina *never* smiled.

'They would hardly guess the truth about *Laddo*, rooming next to Lajjo,' Nina sang blithely mirthlessly. 'Why, we even had connecting doors!'

The mic outside had spluttered to life, over the drone of music, we were suddenly conscious of it.

'And now the finalists ...' the compere's voice rang out.

Lubaina started. 'Hurry, Shilpi,' she said, the urgency transparent for once, in her voice. 'You need to be on stage. C'mon, we have to go.'

'You two better stay quiet,' Lubaina warned us in the same breath as both stepped backward, backing towards the door, still brandishing their knives. 'Not that anyone will hear you over the din outside. You'll be locked in, screaming won't help. And it will get very hot when the flames take over, so save your energy for then.'

'I'll think of you both when I'm wearing the crown,' Nina interjected, her gimlet eyes aglitter. 'Especially *you*, Akruti. Only for a bit though. Later, I'll be too busy conquering Bollywood with SRK. I have to say—it's too bad you both won't be around to witness my moment of glory. It felt nice to tell the tale of our cleverness just now. Won't be the same later. But as they say, change is the only constant. And now, I must be the change.' Nina smiled, a truly enchanting smile if it weren't so absolutely crazed.

Parvati watched them back away, her face still impassive. The torch threw them in shadow as they edged away facing us, their step by step retreat, towards the door. I looked at them leave in growing horror.

Was Nina really so utterly blinded by her ambition that she simply assumed she would be one of the five finalists being called out? How would she go about winning the actual crown? Or had Lubaina, an age-old contest mentor, managed to doctor the final results, somehow? I didn't see how she could have, there was a respected external balloting agency tallying points.

But the reality of our situation hit me abruptly, with terrifying force—we had run out of time and ideas to stop them. In a few seconds, they would be burning the room, along with *us*, down to the ground. Would this really be how it would end for me? Not just the contest, there was so much more I wanted to do with my life. So much more I wanted to be. I hadn't got a chance to tell my parents or Jehaan how much they all meant to me. And now it appeared that I might never be able to ...

I glanced at Parvati in the dim light. Her face was expressionless, almost expectant. I drew myself up tall, taking succour from her icy calmness. If she was being so absurdly brave in the face of assured death—so would I.

There was a sudden movement at the far end. And it wasn't Nina or Lubaina who had moved around there. Before I could see more Parvati had grabbed the torch left on the table upwards and lightning-quick had turned the beam off.

In the darkness, I heard sounds of a scuffle, more heavy seeming than before. Screams, then groans of effort, as if in some sort of desperate clash. Then thuds, one after another, as if two bodies were falling hard. It couldn't be Parvati trying to best Nina once more, she was next to me, switched-off torch in hand. For a nanosecond there was silence yet again in the room. Then an unfamiliar male voice called out, 'Pari—you can switch the torch back on now.'

Zero hour …

30

From the pages of Parvati's diary

9.30 p.m.

I believe I have never loved Brij more than at that moment when he uttered those words to me 'Pari—you can switch the torch back on now!' In one swift movement, he saved Akruti and me from certain and rather painful death by fire. But then, I was at this contest because of him. He had specifically asked it of me, and dutiful as I am, I had agreed to his request!

Anyway, I'll go sequentially with all that happened. I just have to write it all down, the sheer marvel of having something so deeply wrong set right in a trice, just like that, as with a light switch flipped. First up—Akruti's expression. When she saw Brij in the torch beam that I had switched back on, it was as if she's seen a ghost.

'That's the guy,' she whispered to me, panic in her voice. 'The one from the garden, the one who disappeared near the elevators the other day. The one outside our green room today ... he must be with them!'

'Akruti,' I said, as I moved the torch around the room so she had a good look at the immobile Nina and Lubaina, lying collapsed on the floor, unconscious, but not dead, post Brij's intervention. 'I believe he isn't with them.'

I gave her a moment to absorb the scene.

Then, smiling broadly at her shocked face, I added, just to watch her expression, 'And I'd like you to meet Brij. My older brother.'

'How do you do?' Brij came forward, smiling at her, flashing his dimples, now that the danger was at bay.

'The lovely Akruti Rai—in person,' he said. Akruti's face was an absolute picture, but I didn't have time to fully appreciate it. We could hear suddenly, Akruti's name being announced over the mic on stage outside, as a finalist. Followed by mine, to my deepest surprise.

'I believe you may have a contest to win,' Brij told Akruti, stepping aside as she turned to face me, utterly baffled by the turn of events. Then abruptly, as if charged with sudden electricity, she raced out the door to get to the stage.

'You might need to show your face on stage too,' Brij dimpled at me, but I was having none of it.

'You couldn't have come sooner?' I told him, on my way to following Parvati out. 'We might have been killed by these two maniacs.'

'I wouldn't have ever let that happen,' Brij said to me shortly, his voice curt. I believed him. I had staked my life and Akruti's on that fact all this time.

'I know,' I said. Then, as I reached the door, I added: 'You got everything?'

'I think so,' Brij said, as he held up the cassette from the tape recorder I had hidden in the deep recesses of the darkened room. 'Good going, Pari. We have a confession.'

Nina and Lubaina on the floor stirred as they came to, slowly, still disoriented.

'What confession?' Nina asked, she had caught the last part of the conversation.

'*Yours,*' I said to her quietly. 'The one you "felt nice" about telling us, remember? Nina—*you* didn't lead me to you. *I* led you to *me*, by making sure you read my diary that third night. *I* wanted you to hunt me, so I could discover your identity. Sometimes, you see, the hunted *can* become the hunter.'

'Shilpi, Shilpi, Shilpi …' Lubaina was chanting groggily.

'Aunt L? Your daughter is dead!' Nina turned on her, suddenly vicious in defeat. 'My name is *Laddo.*'

I handed Brij the torch, left him to deal with the aftermath of this situation as I raced to the stage. I would not be competing in the final sequence, even though they'd called my name. This was Akruti's dream, not mine, I had raced so fast outside only so I could support her—as she had supported me this entire mess through, despite the fact that her ambition lay elsewhere.

As I reached the wings, I heard the question the judge asked her boom over the mic:

'What two qualities should a Miss India winner most possess?'

Akruti could've said anything—wisdom to save the world, bravery to change it, sympathy, empathy for those less fortunate. But her mind, she later said, only led her to what had transpired seconds before.

She could not forget the fierce pride in Brij's eyes when he looked at me as I introduced them. 'I could not forget you!' she told me. 'That grace under pressure, even as we desperately tried to survive. Your outer calm, masking all that was furiously at play in your mind. A beacon of hope for me in that awful nightmare, whether fighting physically to free us or then appearing to stay passive, even though strategizing internally. The person with me *all the way* in time of danger— all the way, so I *knew it, felt it, was buoyed by it.*'

Akruti smiled at the judge, from onstage, her magnificent gown ablaze in the spotlight. For the first time, free of all the worry and work pressure, I realized the effect her surreal beauty could have on people. Then I heard her answer vibrate through me as she was handed the mic.

'She should possess presence of mind and common sense. So, if heaven forbid, there is darkness, she can lead the way out of it, find the light with ease. Her practicality and good sense a magnet, a moral compass that will help and guide all to stand together as one. After all, don't all roads, all religions, all paths ultimately lead to oneness?

There was complete silence in the amphitheatre, a pin drop silence. Then applause broke out, so thunderous it drowned the music around us. There wasn't a person in the auditorium who didn't know that answer was worthy of the Miss India 1995 crown, though the judges hadn't even marked her on her reply yet. Despite all that had happened, and the later that would follow—tonight would be Akruti's night, after all.

31

Akruti

⌣

That moment, the moment when the compere said 'Miss India 1995 is ... the lovely Akruti Rai!' *that* moment—I'll remember it forever. So many times had I imagined it coming to pass, each time in a different manner, that when it finally truly did—it was almost anti-climatic.

I say almost, because truth be told, I soaked it all in like a grateful sponge, I'll admit it, *every second of it*. This was one dream I'd nurtured and pursued despite all misgiving, all doubt and yes, a trio of murders. Not to mention the risk to my own life and the rather close shave Parvati and I had managed to come through, shaken but miraculously unharmed.

But it *had* happened finally, complete with the glittering crown and the flower bouquet and the confetti and bursting crackers, so pretty out in the open air. And no matter *how* it had happened—I was conscious of the fact that I was now, for a brief spell, very much *in* my best and brightest dream ... *living* it.

Anyone who has ever wanted something badly, and luck and hard work conspire to grant it when that want is yet current they would understand the depth of my feeling. Also that it would outlast the moment. It would be immortalized, imprinted in mind's eye as a sweet spot, forever more. As a guiding light, a ray of sunshine to inspire one's future self, or to compare other victories to, in the days ahead.

To make this time even more special, as I walked my victory lap to the very top of the long ramp, I caught the eye of a very important person in the press box right up front—Jehaan, clapping so hard his hands would be sore the following day. I waved to him and smiled, so the photographer next to him, from *Bharat 360*, got a nice shot … and sashayed back to stage in full 'own the room' mode.

That night though, was a tad bittersweet in a rather bizarre way. Nina, murderous, tipped-over-the-edge Nina, who I had left semi-conscious in the phone room for Parvati's brother Brij to deal with—her idol SRK, Saurav Roop Kamal, also happened to be present at the finale. There as a special guest, in fact, both to be feted himself, as well as to fete the newly crowned Miss India. He hadn't a clue how his very aura had driven a poor girl insane.

'Congratulations,' he smiled at me on the podium, his too-beautiful face alight, as he handed me a bouquet under the lights. I acknowledged his greeting with a tiny smile. I really couldn't bring myself to be more effusive, not right then, thinking of Nina and her warped obsessiveness for him, a passion that had destroyed so many young lives all too quickly. We didn't interact much that night, just posed for the flashbulbs and went our own ways. Later, our paths would cross again, but that story I shall leave for another time.

Not counting that one encounter, the rest of that night was sparkling. A moment of immense personal victory, and I intended to milk it for all it was worth. And apparently it was worth a whole lot, as I found out later that evening.

Parvati located me when I finally had a moment, once the interviews and congratulations were done. Earlier, I had

had an altogether-too brief tête-à-tête with Jehaan, but it was restricted to congratulatory exchanges, I was pulled away almost immediately. Nature of my job, and I knew Jehaan understood perfectly. There would be time enough later for deeper conversations.

My parents, watching the contest live on television from the comfort of their living room, were both proud and emotional when they spoke to me on the phone after. Most gratifying for me, because they too, like Jehaan had come to take my blitzkrieg career for granted for a time.

And dear Avi, the person I owed special thanks to, for his fulsome support and loyalty, such a comfort to me when I had real need of it. Not just overtly, in professional terms, as in his envisioning of my dream dress for the contest. Or placing me centre stage when he could, in ramp sequences, or making sure to check my final prep before the finale. But more so where it counted, when he revealed to me in confidence that the police had found my fingerprints on Lajjo's murder weapon. He need not have, warning a police suspect was risky in that overall atmosphere of suspicion and fear. But he did. And he expressed even more support after telling me, showing me in one move where his trust and allegiance lay. That instance alone, more than all the rest, sealed for me the depth of our bond.

Anyway, we hugged, Avi and I, and shed a few generally fraught tears. It was a big moment after all, in the grand scheme of my modelling career, and he had been my mentor for much of it. Our shared spell of triumph was brief though, as with Jehaan, there were too many people vying for my attention. We would catch up properly later.

In the hurly burly of posing for pictures, I hadn't really met the rest of my fellow contestants after my win either. But

I recall catching my roomie Roxanne's eye, as she filed out with the rest, leaving me to enjoy centre stage as Miss India 1995. And I know what was conveyed in her quick wink was pure goodwill, a joyous camaraderie, as if she was genuinely happy for me. As my roommate, she, more than most, had been witness to both my private and public efforts in securing this title. Saying nothing at all, I knew she understood how much this meant to me.

Now, nearing midnight, I got to go to my room—my private suite, might I add, being the title holder with the crown now—and flopped into a sofa wearily. I actually had a memory flash as I curled up, of my previous room for the last couple of weeks. And in that instant, I missed Roxanne, with her gruff affection, as much as the chaos of the shared floor. Then there was a soft knock on the door, and when I opened it, and Parvati walked in—I was happy I had the suite. More private for all the revelations to follow.

'Congratulations,' Parvati looked at me and smiled, a joyous smile, it lit up her entire face. I noted ruefully that the bruise to her temple from that earlier skirmish with Nina was darker now, in contrast to her light filled demeanour.

'Why didn't you appear for the final round?' I asked her playfully, as I acknowledged her greeting. 'I would've enjoyed the competition.'

'I wanted you to win,' Parvati's smile was sincere, but her eyes shone with mischief. 'You think you would have, had I taken my place in the final five?'

'Doubtful,' I said smiling from ear to ear as I hugged her suddenly. I was only half joking, though I said it lightly. I had already seen what a formidable opponent Parvati made. I much preferred her in my corner, and I knew she was solidly there after all we'd been through.

'Lubaina and Nina?' I asked, conscious of what had been left halfway as we ran out for the Q&A round.

'They're with Addl.CP Mhatre. And Akruti—Tara's free!' Parvati's eyes showed her satisfaction at the turn of events.

'You want to tell me how it is that your brother, someone I never knew even existed, suddenly appeared at exactly the right time, before we became the next statistic on Nina's murder spree?' I said to Parvati. 'And as an aside, I'm most enchanted with your pet name, "Pari"—it means 'angel', I see.'

'More like "fairy", but whatever,' Parvati grinned. 'Simpler to find than *Laddo*.'

'Will they be tried?' I asked, her words recalling the bizarre events that evening.

'More than likely, committed. They clearly need help. You saw that,' Parvati's expression was serious. Then she added: 'Akruti—my brother is part of RAW. I was here because he asked me to be.'

I understood at once what a big confidence she was entrusting me with. Families of RAW agents, especially if they know their relatives are part of it, don't go around saying so. One of the basics of RAW is secrecy, so Jehaan told me.

'Not because of your burning ambition to win the crown?' I kept it light, and I could see that she was grateful for that.

'That too,' Parvati smiled. 'Only so I could be one up on *you*.' We both laughed at her understatement, this girl who had even been called on stage as part of the final five and had casually skipped the opportunity for a shot at the title.

'Brij was informed of some suspicious activity taking place in an international company, under the guise of being a sponsor for this event,' Parvati continued. 'You know a lot about RAW involves counter-terrorism and espionage, don't you?'

'Yes,' I watched Parvati, wondering how much she was allowed to reveal, or whether she was overstepping in her effort to do right by me.

'He didn't tell me much himself, he isn't allowed to,' Parvati went on. 'But he suggested, in the inimitable way he has, that I might want to take part in the Miss India contest this year. Report anything or anyone I might find suspicious. He didn't believe there would be any danger in the contest itself, because it was the sponsors that were under scrutiny. But he also told me that if there was, he'd be here to make sure I'd be safe.'

'I see,' I said. I *did* see. Parvati was here on RAW work as Jehaan had rightly guessed, only it wasn't for her super powerful father. It was for her influential brother, also RAW.

'Imagine his surprise then, when serial murders started happening,' Parvati continued. 'At the contest he'd sent his baby sister, the pampered pet in the family, to participate in … the contest he'd thought would be safe enough!'

'But they weren't linked?' I asked, trying to find a connect between the antics of Nina and Lubaina, and a possible terror alert situation courtesy the suspicious activity of a bogus sponsor.

'Not at all. Sheer, crazy coincidence,' Parvati said. 'There was no danger from the sponsor end at this contest. Brij's earlier concern, the reason he asked me to take part, never materialized. This situation was independent of it. Trust a grieving mother, driven mad by the loss of her only child, and trying to make up for it by substituting her niece, to create havoc such as cannot be imagined …'

'To take lives,' I added quietly. 'Murder innocents in cold blood.'

'What mothers won't do for their children at the most normal of times,' Parvati said simply. 'You have to allow though, for the fact that Lubaina wasn't normal.'

'Nor Nina,' I concurred. 'She was the one who actually struck the blow each time. Lajjo, Doreen and Nuzhat ... all by her hand. And would've been us too, but for your brother. Ironic, how he had you here investigating the possibility of suspicious activity, and I thought of *him* as a suspect! On more than one occasion!'

'Honestly, Akruti, the timing of his coming was serendipitous, especially at the very end when we were being locked in that room. I had run out of ideas to save us! I realized after a bit, that it was him you were describing earlier. Though I hadn't seen him myself, not even a glimpse at the elevator that one time,'Parvati smiled. 'I had to get you off his trail till he was ready to reveal himself.'

'And is he?' I asked, curious.

'Are they ever?' Parvati smiled. 'The most I got was the fact that he managed to turn off all the lights on the premises just before the finale! He was here, of course, you saw him outside the green room before the finale. He's been here since news of the first murder broke. The day you saw him at the garden, he had just come in. He'd promised to keep me safe, but I was hell bent on solving this, I wanted to stay and he couldn't change my mind on phone. So he flew in, though I didn't see him at all—*you* did!

At the finale, he trailed behind to the phone room, saw Nina follow me there. I knew whoever *Laddo* was, she'd read the diary again. She'd try and hunt me down before or during the finale if my diary, or rather, my *pursuit* of *Laddo*'s identity was dangerous to her. I deliberately came back to my room that last night with the diary, locked it in my drawer. Sure enough Tania took it for Nina and she read it. I was right, she wanted me out of the picture.

Brij got all the lights to go off when he realized the situation I would soon be in. He waited till Nina went upstairs for a torch and slipped me the cassette recorder to hide in the interim, so I could tape any confession. This was when I knew at last, that my guess, of Brij being here as the man you'd kept seeing, had been correct. It was very hurried, meeting him for the first time at the contest in this way, so much was at stake. Then, as Nina mentioned, and I acknowledged, I *waited* till her return in that room, in the darkness. But not *for* her—for her *confession*. Brij and I, we both knew what followed next would be dangerous.

He could've stopped me, but he went with my instincts though he knew it was a gamble. A scary one too, because Nina had killed many times before. But I was determined. Imagine my surprise and fear for your safety when you landed up!'

'Parvati …' I said, not being able to speak further, overcome at Parvati's quiet fortitude. I wondered if I would go this far, stay knowingly with a crazy person in a dark room, for a confession, at the risk of my life. My appearance there all of a sudden must've really played on Parvati's conscience. She could gamble with her own life—mine was another matter!

'The only hitch' Parvati continued lightly, ignoring my emotional interjection. 'I wasn't sure Brij would save us in time, it was so dark throughout. I didn't know if he'd managed to see Lubaina enter, guess her involvement, or to guess that both had knives with them. Or that they intended to torch us in the room!'

'Good for us both siblings operate so on instinct, then!' I said to her, bringing much needed levity to a conversation much too heavy by half.

'Lubaina's involvement was a shock, even for me,' Parvati smiled at my comment, then continued, grim-faced. 'She came out of nowhere, and held the key to all. But Brij managed to save the day, despite all nasty surprises.'

'Did Nina, if she managed to get rid of us, really have a shot at the crown?' I asked Parvati, recalling my earlier musings in the phone room. 'Was she slated to be part of the final five? Could she have actually become Miss India?'

'The tabulation for this contest is not done by *Eye India*, but by an external balloting agency—you know this,' Parvati's voice was gentle. 'Even if Lubaina wanted to help her win using some measure of influence, I doubt she could have. Both aunt and niece were living in an altered reality.'

'And the Addl.CP?' I was curious. 'Did he know why you were here?'

'No, but he knew whose daughter and sister I was,' Parvati said, somewhat ruefully. 'He is high enough on the hierarchy to have found out that there was more at play than meets the eye, hence my presence at the contest. He might not have known specifics. Then, when the killings began, he would have realized that whatever else I was, I was no suspect, nor murderer. Nor anyone that I chose to be friends with!'

'Oh!' I caught what she was implying and realised one more of her many kindnesses had been to provide a vital, if imperceptible immunity for me. No wonder the Addl.CP had dragged his feet about arresting me, despite my fingerprints on the blade that killed Lajjo.

Her father and brother had already run background checks on me before Parvati approached me for help at the very beginning itself, I had no doubt on that. But why dwell on it? She had been a protector and provided support when I needed her most, especially on that night Lajjo fell in my arms, already approaching rigor mortis. And Parvati continued to be so, all through till the end, whether I realised it or not. For that I needed only to be grateful.

'Thank you, Parvati,' I said suddenly.

'Thank *you*, Akruti,' Parvati's eyes twinkled, as she replied to me in the same vein.

We stood looking at each other, slightly awkward at the intensity of the moment.

Then Parvati broke the spell. 'You saw how the Addl.CP left us alone, no matter what we went to him with! Clearly floored by your good looks, grace and winsome intelligence!'

We both laughed. The Addl.CP had known Parvati's background, given us immunity we were not even aware of, or rather, I wasn't, no matter how surreal the situation. Very rarely does that happen.

All along I had wondered why he allowed two girls to pretty much have their way, even assisted us without seeming to, like showing us that video recording of the rehearsal the night Lajjo was killed. Now I knew.

'Shall we celebrate our continuing existence on this earth?' Parvati asked tongue-in-cheek. 'Or then, your wonderful conquest of the glitterbug crown?'

'Both,' I told her, suddenly fiercely joyful, looking for the champagne, in this fancy suite I'd been allotted. 'Let's do both!'

⌒

'So your dream, that nightmare … it was actually a portent, wasn't it?' Jehaan, speaking to me later that night seemed utterly serious over the phone, but I could sense the underlying mischief waiting to surface. 'Reality played out something like that, didn't it?'

'I guess,' I said thoughtfully. 'Nina really *did* want the crown, so it was actually a shadowy Miss India hopeful who was behind the murders …'

'I didn't mean Nina,' Jehaan said, then broke into that all-out guffaw he was holding back. 'I meant *you*! You wanted that title so much, you dreamed of yourself, as a ghoul after a hoary crown, ha, ha, ha!'

'I really don't think that's funny, Jeh,' I told him. 'You can make all the pathetically poor jokes possible. But it won't make me forget how very troubled I was by all that was happening then. Enough to have nightmares, as you well know!'

'It's strange, we were aided by serendipitous coincidences often enough,' I continued my conversation with him, now thoughtful. 'Whether you acknowledge them or not. As Avi's calling the police in immediately when Lajjo was stabbed, not waiting for *Eye India* to dither or try to cover up that stabbing. Or his changing the music at rehearsal at the last minute, so the drug given to Lajjo didn't come into effect at the time Nina-Lubaina had hoped it would. Or my own impulsive decision to walk ramp from the front that night, so I escaped being thought of as the one who stabbed Lajjo from the back, even though I was included as a suspect. Or me chancing upon Gokul unexpectedly backstage before the finale, and him giving me *Laddo*'s real name just like that. Or, Brij's arrival *exactly* when we needed him to come at the end—he saved us from being burned alive. Or then, my nightmare itself … you may make fun of me now, but it was *you* who pointed out at the time, that it was my subconscious trying to direct me to *a contestant* as suspect. You were right.'

'It's a rocker of a front page story tomorrow,' Jehaan, trying to be contrite, shared his barely-contained excitement on the next day's headlines-to-be. 'Glamour, gore, greed … in true tradition of maniacal criminals—tomorrow's will be a sell-out story for all media.'

'Glad I could make your day,' I countered drily, still not in a forgiving mood.

'Oh, you *always* make my day, Aku,' the irrepressible Jehaan charm was at 100-watt supra sparkle now. 'But tomorrow? Tomorrow, you and your friend Parvati—you'll be making the nation's!'

Epilogue
Akruti

And really, that's how it came to be, the trigger for my current profession. It was as Jehaan predicted, all the way and it blew us away by how fast it all happened. The next day's headlines were only the beginning to a tight, dizzyingly steep, vertical climb up as far as our public profiles went. And it went on and on.

We were lauded for our presence of mind, our bravery and our quick thinking. Parvati's RAW connections were not spoken of, naturally. But for that tight circle of powers-that-be in the uppermost echelons of the nation's influentials, the 'think-tank' doers as it were—she became a precious asset. Not the least for her youth and freshness as for her clarity of purpose and her impressive lineage.

We won numerous accolades, perhaps more weighty, if not more prized than my Miss India title. That, despite all the ones to follow, would always hold a very special place in my heart.

I should confess here that after all I had gone through to bag this title, my original goal in pursuing it—an easy entry into Bollywood didn't seem as appealing. Everything had changed, bringing in the temptation of newer, more fulfilling possibilities. The option of a far more challenging, if not more lucrative vocation beckoned. My horizons had opened up beyond belief, in a direction I could never have imagined in my wildest dreams.

Meanwhile Parvati's diary became quite the showpiece. It is kept in the *Eye India* archives now, for any Miss India hopeful to gawk at, living proof of a time when they almost had to cancel their national treasure contest. This, but for a girl who was determined to help right things and her ambitious comrade-in-arms (who was equally determined to win things!). So we are driven by what we desire deep within, and if committed enough, we are victorious, (sash, crown 'n all!).

And that is how also, we are often brought on the path we were meant to follow all along. And that is how it happened for us as well.

'Why don't you cement it,' one of our well-meaning friends remarked in casual conversation one day. 'Make it official? Become who you are already known as? Become ... *hope*?' I think what she said struck a rather deep chord in us both. We liked the idea of becoming ... hope.

Somehow all those coincidences I had described to Jehaan, happenstances as they were, but aiding us along our journey of discovery—we believed they were meant to help us become *more*. By then we had already become 'Aku' and 'Pari' to each other. I don't think we ever again used our full names in addressing each other as we formally had the entire pageant through.

Anyway, with Parvati's zealous brand of energy, no sooner decided, than done. Licences were looked into that evening, an office was allotted fairly quickly. And one fine day, I arrived at work, not to walk on a wooden ramp, and pout as I had been accustomed to, but to a tastefully shiny wooden desk, under an office placard that read simply but proudly: '*Akruti and Parvati. Private Investigators*'.

And thus it came to be that my chance encounter with the Bollywood superstar SRK led to him offering us our first case in our business together. But as I said, that story is for another telling.

What lay ahead would not be easy. Not entirely as glamorous as what I'd been used to thus far, either. But it would most certainly not be boring!

Cut to the present, 2018

So many years have passed since then, so much has happened in the interim. I am now matronly perhaps, for all my diva status of yore, and for all my niece Niamat's ego boost, called me her 'glamorous auntie Aku'. Young women like Niamat look up to me, not just as future Miss India hopefuls, I think, but as inspiration to pursue any dream that fills them with hope and light and wonder, despite the grimness and hardship involved in reaching it.

We are still a team, Parvati and I. Since that initial success we have managed to cement ourselves in the national psyche as go-tos for complicated conundrums. As our reputation grew and prospered, we got our hands on some really intriguing mysteries together—and tried hard to live up to the reason we had started our agency together in the first place: 'become hope'. Did we succeed? We'd like to believe we did, in some measure.

Suffice to say, today when people talk of the Akruti Rai, it is mostly *not* as an iconic model that they place me. More probable, they are registering me as one half of the rather well entrenched Indian Private Investigator duo, 'Akruti and

Parvati', the international brand. Yes, we are now global in reach in 2018, thanks to the times we live in, so different from 1995, our first case together!

I watch Niamat with pride as she pirouettes once more on stage, chasing her future. It had all gone awry in 1995 as I chased mine. And, of course, it may have been sheer bumbling luck that carried us safely forward then.

But somehow, more than serendipitous coincidences, I believe it was our conviction to help, to make right those awful atrocities *in any way we could.* Despite our inexperience, or age or circumstance—*to be the best version of ourselves we could possibly be*—that delivered us to safety in the end.

Not just safety—for me, a whole new career track, a whole new world. It opened up just like that, because I dared to dream as true to self, as big as I did, in the face of such extreme odds.

You could say our world view determined our destiny. And for that, I wish such a dream of conquest on all who chose to believe, both in dreams (of pageants and crowns or otherwise), as much in *themselves* as talismans of hope, of *rightness* in an oft-unsafe world. As for us, we got plenty of opportunities to try and live up to that notion we began our business together with—of being, of becoming *hope* to those who asked … but that as they say, is another story!

Acknowledgements

Nothing exists in a vacuum, thank you and thank you for your support and generosity in this journey...

Chaitanya: There are no words big enough to encompass your generosity of spirit, that largesse that fills every void. I don't think a 'thank you' would quite cover how special you are to me. But I have to begin somewhere, so let me say not the least for troll and demon duty, hauling both to work in the long hot summer, so I could write in peace.

Jyotsna and **Suresh:** Papa and ma, thank you your unquestioning support. And for babysitting both the two-legged and the four-legged grandchildren, whilst I wrote and Chait travelled.

Tariecka and **Raphael:** For that uncomplicated, joyous love that forgives all my trespasses. For existing.

My gracious in-laws, **Leena** and **Pushpendra**, for restful intervals at The House on the Farm, Chait's wonderland extraordinaire, which birthed my first sentence, as it did my final read.

Arjun Gaind: A conversation, an idea, my resignation with stereotypes, till that suggestion, turning experience on its head, and then—*this*. I am deeply grateful for your many kindnesses, as for your unrelenting encouragement. And will always value all the advice you so big-heartedly shared.

Manasi Subramaniam: For initiating this cycle. It was you who set the wheels in motion, easily and quickly, I am ever grateful for that.

Roshni Olivera: For being that sensible and wise sounding board every single time I hit a curveball. And for offering vital advice. I am truly thankful you are in my life.

Soumyadipta Banerjee: Intrepid Crime reporter, ally— my go-to guy for detailing processes in criminal procedures and national secret agencies that serve this wonderful nation of ours. Thank you.

Manish Pachouly: Veteran Crime journalist, thank you for helping me understand Law and Order hierarchy in beloved Mumbai.

Ananth Padmanabhan and HarperCollins for their faith in my book, thank you so much!

Diya Kar Hazra and the dynamic team at Harper, for supportiveness through this book's birthing and addressing all worries promptly, with thoughtfulness, a big thank you!

And *most* especially to the wonderful *Swati Daftuar*, for being the kind of editor one hopes for but seldom manages to find. Thank you, *so* very much for your sensitivity, patience, indulgence and above all—inspired editing. It has been such a joy to work with you.